PROMISE RING

PROMISE RING

A STORY ABOUT LIFE CHOICES

A NOVEL

BONNIE BEECH
Author of *Dinosaur Mountain*

iUniverse, Inc.
New York Lincoln Shanghai

Promise Ring
A Story about Life Choices

Copyright © 2007 by Bonnie Beech

All rights reserved. No part of this book may be used or reproduced by any means, graphic, electronic, or mechanical, including photocopying, recording, taping or by any information storage retrieval system without the written permission of the publisher except in the case of brief quotations embodied in critical articles and reviews.

iUniverse books may be ordered through booksellers or by contacting:

iUniverse
2021 Pine Lake Road, Suite 100
Lincoln, NE 68512
www.iuniverse.com
1-800-Authors (1-800-288-4677)

Because of the dynamic nature of the Internet, any Web addresses or links contained in this book may have changed since publication and may no longer be valid.

This is a work of fiction. All of the characters, names, incidents, organizations, and dialogue in this novel are either the products of the author's imagination or are used fictitiously.

ISBN: 978-0-595-41842-8 (pbk)
ISBN: 978-0-595-86184-2 (ebk)

Printed in the United States of America

To Bill,
If only they met you half-way.

ACKNOWLEDGEMENTS

To my family, may we know in our hearts that we love each other even though outside forces have kept us apart. May we, in the future, stand up to these outside forces and put each other first. To my father, who in sadness has placed his work above his family. May he know that even though he can't take the money with him, that the only thing that matters is that he seeks God once again in his life and know that getting back on the path is simple, say a prayer. To my mother, who sought refuge in another and caused a domino effect for our family. We forgive you. I just wish dad would. Maybe then the family would have a chance at healing. I love you for your intuition, faith and wanting only the best for me and John. For my BFF, Allison. You've always believed in me and I would hate to lose that with the writing of this book. I hope that you know you will always be my BFF and I should've named my first daughter after you as you know I meant to. To Cindy, thank-you for letting me ask Bill, although you could've probably handled him better. Thank-you also for being there for me and letting me be a part of your family when mine wasn't around. To my first editor, Darla Bruno. Thank-you so much for your tough love. This book went through many changes and name changes because of your wonderful editing style. I wouldn't have had any other editor help me and the fact that you are from Jersey helped all the more. To Brenda Kluck and iuniverse.com. You have opened a door for me that I was too stubborn to have closed. I want to thank-you for your patience and year-long help on the many changes this book went through. Brenda, you have truly walked me through each and every step and given me insight as to how difficult getting a book completed to perfection really is. I thank you for your dedication in helping me with this project. I would like to thank all of my friends in high school. Each and everyone of you in the Class of '82 helped me make the choice to stay and work my way through to graduation day. We were that close and I would never think of going to a different school. To my high school, may you help those children who are suffering from their parent's divorce. I had no guidance, yet I graduated from one of the best colleges in California. Last, but not least, I would like to thank my husband, Adrian for his patience in letting me write about Bill. There are no words to state the amount of love that I have for you. You are my life and my love, although not my first love, I need you to survive each day. To my children, William, Alice and Kaitlyn, you are a blessing to me in which I pray each day, thank-ful that you are all in my life. Lastly, I would like to thank Pam, my mentor in my profession and BFF. You've been there for me through everything and the best thing about it … we've had a lot of fun!

CHAPTER ONE
BIRTHDAY CELEBRATION

My name is Pamela. I am a typical California girl, born and raised there, who just graduated from high school. Uncertain about my future, I opt to live my life in the moment. Uncertainty is risky for the new high school graduate. One moment, there I am hanging out with my friends happily enjoying the social aspects of high school. The next moment I am working frantically as a cashier at a department store so that I could pay my school tuition. You see, my parents wanted me to stop going to the private high school. They wanted me to attend the more affordable public high school that my neighbors attended. I adamantly said to them in typical adolescent fashion, "No way." I wanted to graduate with my friends, that being the major goal in my life for the past two years. It's not that my parents were too poor, it's that they divorced during my sophomore year of high school. I worked my way through the last two years of high school because of my parents' ignorance on how to salvage their eighteen-year marriage and their apparent hatred for each other's actions that led to the divorce. It's not that I didn't enjoy working at the department store part time after school; I did enjoy learning the tricks of the trade of commercialism. It's the fact that I didn't have enough time to dedicate to achieving academic success, therefore ironically, almost not getting to graduate with my friends due to suffering grades. My grades suffered because school just wasn't a priority for me. Social activities were a priority because I had no parental supervision to direct me otherwise. Working part time was not the only reason why my grades suffered. Other factors like fretting over my boyfriend's whereabouts also played a role. Bill, my boyfriend, was making me suffer emotionally. He dumped me like a hot potato, but never officially broke up with me. I was still in love with him, but he seemed to want to explore other possibilities, thus dating other people. Yes, uncertainty was a factor in my life, in that I didn't quite know or care what the future might hold. I knew that I had no business applying to a university like some of my other classmates would, so I opted to enroll at the local community college. I would attend exercise classes in the fall. In the meantime, I was to enjoy my summer after graduation. The first celebration on my agenda came when my mother offered to take me to my eighteenth birthday celebration in late June to a French restaurant in Santa Barbara. Santa Barbara is a city located thirty-five miles north of the city where I spent my adolescent life, Ventura. Santa Barbara is aptly named the American Riviera, because the weather is similar to that of the French Riviera on the Mediteranian Sea. The weather isn't the only good thing about Santa Barbara. The city's scenic nature, with the Santa Ynez Mountains as a backdrop and the Pacific Ocean views of many of the architecturally designed white houses with terra cotta–tiled roofs, make this a popular city for tourists around the world. The streets are tree lined and clean, no billboards destroying the beauty of the landscape. I spent my eighteenth birthday with my mother and her boyfriend, Maurice, at a charming French restaurant. El Encanto is perched high on the hills above Santa Barbara, where the views of the city below and ocean are amazing. Santa Barbara and its charming Mediterranean ambience, is a city in which I was honored to commemorate my birthday. A place and time where I could forget about the aspects of what my future would hold, if not for a couple hours before I would be back to reality trying to figure out what direction life would take me.

My mother found El Encanto by accident. She and Maurice had gotten lost in the hills on the way to the Santa Barbara Mission and Natural History Museum, turned left into the El Encanto, and ended up having "the best dinner in the most beautiful dining room I've ever seen." "Wait until you see it," my mother told me, effusively describing the candlelit tables, the view of the city below, and the hotel's famous lily pond. She launched into an excited description of the restaurant's outdoor garden and the wisteria that clambered up the pergola wall: "Did you know that some varieties of wisteria are edible? They use it in salads. You can even use it to make wine ... the El Encanto uses fresh, local ingredients ..." my mother trailed off, blushing at her own enthusiasm. "I want you to feel like you're in France. Wait until you taste their escargots. They're amazing!"

I looked suspiciously at my mother, who seemed to not be able to wait to teach me a few lessons on French culture. "What are escargots?"

My mother looked at me, giggling. "They're edible snails. But you'll like them! When you visit France this summer you can compare them to the ones we'll have at your birthday dinner."

I stuck out my tongue. "Yuck. I'll never try snails."

"Yes, you will," she responded calmly, "and I bet you like them, too. Please don't make any comments until you've tasted one. The chef serves them with garlic butter, and you love garlic."

I frowned. I was going to be eighteen—an adult—and supposed it was time to develop more sophisticated tastes. "I guess part of growing up is being open to trying new things."

The planning that went into this dinner was a stark contrast to my sixteenth birthday, which I had spent alone at home wondering why my parents wouldn't buy me a car. This dinner signified the positive changes that were taking place in my life. It was one of the best celebrations I'd ever had. I was as enthusiastic about the elegant, candlelit restaurant as my mother had been. We arrived early enough to get a glimpse of the pond.

I was in awe from the moment I walked in to the hotel lobby, silently taking in the shiny wooden floors, the huge portraits hanging on the walls, the mahogany furniture, and crystal-infused glasswork dividing the rooms. The dining area had a French feel to it, with light green trim and curtains above the French doors. Natural sunlight enveloped the west side of the restaurant, making the room bright and warm. Today was nothing like the birthdays I'd experienced in the past. I'd learned not to expect excessive and lavish gifts as I had received on birthdays as a child. Knowing those days were over, I was trying to feel genuine gratitude for any glimmer of what might be mistaken for indulgence.

The only thing I missed that night was Bill's lighthearted voice. His absence caused a lump in my throat that I tried to attribute to the quickly swallowed snail I had ventured to taste. The drive home to Ventura included a luminous view of the moon shining over the Pacific Ocean and the oil rigs standing in the distance, their lights making them seem like they were lined up for a parade. Bill worked on one of those oil rigs, although I wasn't sure which. I hadn't heard from him in a while and was wondering if he was working tonight. I told myself that he was, or else he certainly would have been with me on my birthday. I was beginning to feel calm and peaceful, a respite from my recent state of perplexed pessimism—lack of direction. Driving south along Highway 101, after having a remarkable dinner, I felt sleepy and at peace with the world. I had no inkling of the tragic news the next day would bring.

CHAPTER TWO
EMPLOYMENT AGENCY

Bill was my first love. I'd met him a couple of weeks after he moved from Rochester, New York, to complete his senior year of high school in Ventura. I was working as a part-time cleaning person for a woman whose husband had died. I was only fifteen years old, and this was my second job. My first had been babysitting for the neighbor kids when I was twelve, old enough to babysit. This new job, which I could only do on the weekends because I was a freshman in high school, gave me some added responisiblity. My parents wanted me to be more responsible, especially since I would be turning sixteen that June: my father thought I should work so I could start saving for a car. I agreed with my father. I needed to be a more responsible person, especially if being responsible meant getting a car, so I called an employment agency I'd heard about through one of my friends. I met Bill during my first job placement. He and his mother lived in a converted upstairs apartment my boss owned. I was a bit reluctant to take the first job the employment service offered me: I was a suspicious person. I thought to myself, "Why am I so suspicious, so afraid of the types of jobs the employment agency will offer me?" I knew that my shy nature had to do with my reluctance at accepting positions.

Because of my shyness, I asked my friend Cynthia if she would come with me to help ease my fear of meeting new people and accepting new jobs. I dreaded the awkward moments I imagined, made up my mind to call her. Cynthia and I met a couple of years before. We attended a private Christian school in Ventura. I walked to school every day because my parents were more attentive to their careers than to their children. The gray Cadillac would pass by as I walked, two blond haired, blue-eyed girls waving at me from the rear window. Yes, I really wanted a ride, and I was grateful when the alluring car finally stopped in front of me one winter's day. But I remembered my mother's words, "Don't ever get in a stranger's car," and I was reluctant to approach. I figured, however, that these were students who attended the same school as me, so my attitude quickly changed. After an awkward climb into the backseat, I soon felt like a princess who was being chauffeured. "There was nothing to be worried about," I thought to myself. From that day forward, I enjoyed the attentiveness of my new friend's mother and her frequent rides to and from school.

I spent an hour standing in my bedroom trying to decide if I should ask my friend to go with me to the job. When I finally got up the nerve to pick up the phone, Cynthia's mother offered not only let Cynthia venture out with me, but to also drive us to my weekend place of employment. Even she had second thoughts when we arrived, saying, "I don't know about this. Would you rather me drop you off and wait while you help the lady clean her house?" I felt that the new situation and the fact that we were going into a stranger's home made everyone involved feel on edge.

"Don't worry," I told Cynthia's mom, "the employment service has worked with this woman in the past, and you know where we are. Hopefully, she'll let us use her phone to call you when we're done." This was before cell phones were common, so I certainly hoped she would.

"What's this job going to be like?" I wondered, avoiding Cynthia's irritated look. The older woman, Mary, who answered the door, looked down at us with authority. The employment agency warned warned me not to expose too much personal information at the various assignments. I thought back to the numerous tax and legal papers that I had signed, rules I had read. My personality was cautious, but jovial, too. I liked to talk. I had nothing to fear. I was a well-rounded individual who came from a good home. I couldn't understand why I couldn't divulge personal information to a woman who looked as if she lived in isolation for years, possibly needing a shoulder to cry on or an ear to capture. I'm sure that the stories of her past would be abundant, and that she would welcome us as company and as possible confidants. I wanted to follow the strict instructions of the employment agency, but found myself also wanting to ease this woman's pain and heartache. I entered her beautiful home delivering an internal reprimand to myself: I can't compare her life to mine. I need to follow the instructions of the employment agency or I won't get a good reference.

Part of me was longing to find out the history of the house. It placed a sort of spell on me. I looked at the eye-opening minimalist pictures on the wall, deciding that the home didn't seem to have been decorated by the lunatic I had imagined in my moments of insecurity. I turned my gaze to the mistress of the house, who appeared equally well put together. Her personal style wasn't that of a woman trying to seduce a man, those years far behind her. She didn't seem to care about fashion trends or impressing people. Her personal style seemed quick and easy—she wore no jewelry and was dressed in loose-fitting trousers and a blue chambray long-sleeved cotton shirt. Her look was far from frumpy, her hair neatly wrapped in a tight bun, her skin flawless. The woman was dressed in menswear chic, capturing something of Kate Hepburn's classic masculine style.

As we made our grand entrance, the lady of the house greeted us with, "I only paid for one of you."

I replied that I brought my friend so that she could help me be more efficient in cleaning the large house.

The lady must have guessed at my fears of a bad reference, because she allowed Cynthia to stay with me that day. Tomorrow, she said, I would have to come alone. "This is for legal reasons," she told me, "I only signed documents for one girl." I decided that she was unpleasantly stubborn and set in her ways.

I could always go back to babysitting the neighbor kids, I thought, although I knew that leaving wouldn't be an option. I needed to save money for a car.

She went on to explain that she would be entertaining and had been busy putting party favors and dinner place cards on the table before we arrived. Her table was decorated with inspiration because the table settings were modern, and I started wondering if her past employment included included working for a fashion designer. She took her silver out from its case and asked me to shine it. She pointed to her china cabinet and continued, "After you're through shining the silver, I'll need you to take each crystal martini and champagne glasses out and make sure that there are no water spots. I put them in the dishwasher last night, but I want everything to look spectacular when my guests arrive. This is going to be a special evening."

I looked at the dining area and hoped she wasn't going to have us dust the chandelier. I blurted out my admiration for the vintage light fixture—"that's gorgeous!. My mother has one just like it!"—I then remembered that it was a cardinal sin to discuss your personal life with your employer. I blushed, knowing that I had broken the first of many commandments in this woman's lonely asylum.

After giving us our first instructions and a short tour of the downstairs portion of her home, the lady went on to deliver a stern warning: "I don't want any funny stuff going on here. I need you to work quietly, because I've rented out the upstairs portion of my home. I'm a single woman on a fixed income, and I need the money. I don't want you two girls to run off my renters."

I rebutted as politely as I could, thanking her for letting me bring Cynthia and adding meekly, "we'll do our best to do exactly what you instructed and keep the renters in mind." I felt oddly grown up and childishly fearful at the same time. I knew that I couldn't get carried away by my imagination, but knowing there were strangers living upstairs made me feel a little bit on edge because I was afraid of being alone with the lady. Having strangers upstairs made me more afraid of being alone with her. I couldn't understand why Mary would want to have people living above her.

As we cleaned the silver and crystal, the woman explained her rules for entertaining. "One can't be a good hostess without party music," she began, and told us that she had purchased an old phonograph at a garage sale. She would be playing old Frank Sinatra and Benny Goodman records. I glanced at my friend, trying not to chuckle. My grandmother used to watch Benny Goodman; our own current playlist featured Madonna, Cindy Lauper, and Pat Benetar. I doubted this woman would want our advice when it came to entertainment music. She then talked about how she found the catering service: She was swimming laps at the YMCA when she heard another customer praising their carrot-mint soup. The carrot soup, the elegant table, and the centerpiece of orchids from the Carpinteria coast all struck me as luxurious but intimate touches. I decided that she must have a pretty good life after all.

Cynthia and I were both relieved when we finished cleaning her designer stemware and silver, placing each above the Lenox china place settings that sat upon the silk tablecloth. I bent over to smell the orchids, thinking, "What would a dinner party be without flowers?" I thought about how my mother set the table for her own parties. My mother loved giving dinner parties, had done so my entire life. I myself had yet to learn many "womanly" arts such as sewing, knitting, or entertaining. Little did I know that this woman's home would be the setting for some of the most educational events of my life—the art of seduction being one of the most important learning experiences. I sat at her dining table, starring at the brilliant crystal, wondering what my future would entail. I could never have guessed that my whimsical, romantic imaginings would ultimately have such an effect on my future. I was too young to know how to make them real, or to predict what might happen if I did. But I was open to experimenting.

CHAPTER THREE
THE ETHEREAL INFLUENCE

I woke early the next day, apprehension about facing the job alone making my stomach churn. I decided that breakfast might help and put on my robe and slippers. The cold water I splashed on my face relieved the bizarre feeling I was having. It would be a miracle if I got through this day without one of my trademark anxiety attacks. One of the contributors to these attacks was the fact that I was forever trying to figure out people in general. I embarked on a never-ending quest to be the best, the most stylish, and the hottest teenager on the planet. I wanted to look like I'd just walked off the runway at Bloomingdale's, and I had in fact been a teenage model at a department store. I was tall and thin, and the event's organizers kept telling me I had a future in modeling. I coveted the dress the store let me borrow for the event—I felt beautiful in it because it was made of fabric that made my skin tingle. Unfortunately, when I actually found myself onstage, in front of an audience of hundreds, I couldn't stop spinning in circles. When I got back to the dressing room, not surprisingly, the mood changed. A woman came up to me and practically grabbed the dress off of my back, asking in angry bewilderment why I couldn't walk straight down the catwalk. I didn't know. I looked at her and started crying. It seemed that my anxiety attacks had started at that moment.

My mother picked me up backstage, saying, "Honey, you were great!"

Looking resentfully at the women still talking about me in the corner, I muttered, "they said I was horrible."

My mother looked at them, and before I knew it she had walked over and demanded the dress I'd worn on the catwalk.

The petite, French-speaking woman who taught the modeling class told her it was hanging up: "we want our dresses to stay fresh, so we take them off of the models the minute they get back."

My mother walked over to the dress and removed it from the hanger, saying, "I'd like to purchase the dress for my daughter." I knew then that my mother was on a quest to make me feel I was the best model on stage.

I walked over to my closet and opened the wooden doors with their floor length mirrors. I found the dress, and suddenly I was in a lighter mood. This dress was not only beautiful, but I felt almost as if it had a life of its own—or at least as if I took on a new liveliness when I wore it. I knew I would wear it someday; I just didn't know when. There were school dances and other formal social events coming up, and the dress would be perfect. The only problem was that I didn't have a candidate to accompany me to these important milestones. Dreaming about attending the next dance in the blue Jessica McClintock frock, I placed it neatly back in the closet and closed the doors. I had a feeling that I would be celebrating the dress's debut in the near future.

Reality hit me like a tornado. I committed to a job that seemed impossible to complete, and I knew that it would be beneficial to use my time wisely to prepare for the day ahead. Given the frequency in which Mary mentioned her fixed income and her need for the tenants' rent money, I thought it was odd that she was having us clean her crystal and silver for an upcoming dinner. I then remembered that she also wanted me to help her with her renter's laundry. Washing and folding strangers' laundry didn't appeal to me. I could easily think of several more pleasing ways to spend my day, but I made a commitment. I thought to myself that I was going to have to find better ways to come up with money. But my personal assets were few, and I knew perfectly well that my disdain for such work was futile. I felt vaguely that my transition into decorous adulthood was being warped by my need to fit in at school, at work, and in love. My need for love was quite uncivilized and unyielding, even though—or maybe precisely because—I was still a cautious young girl of fifteen. I was terrified by the new territory I would have to enter to begin my metamorphosis into an adult woman, but it was a fascinated kind of terror. At another level, it seemed that my sole purpose in life was to misbehave with the opposite sex.

Later that morning I rang my employer's doorbell, reluctantly beginning another day at the mercy of a meticulous, meddlesome old lady. I coaxed Cynthia into returning with me, even though the lady had expressly forbidden her to do so. Even with a friend to protect me, though, I thought longingly of simply turning around and walking away—it wouldn't be the first time I had relinquished my responsibilities. I babysat for a family down the street for months. They were kind and paid me well. I shared my duties with my next-door neighbor. When they moved, I was heartbroken. I had grown close to the kids—and I enjoyed having my own money. The new owners of their house offered me work, but they also offered me a precise and restricted portion of food to eat during my time at the house, set out alongside a detailed list of what I could and couldn't do. Not only had the owners changed, but so had the job itself. I decided not to show up one night when I'd agreed to babysit. Instead, I sat at home watching television with my brother and father, ignoring the phone as it rang off the hook. When I ignored my father's lecture on my irresponsibility and his irritable admonitions to answer the phone, he considered me with disappointed disbelief, wondering aloud why I wouldn't at least let the people know I wouldn't be coming over. Still, I opted to ignore my responsibilities. Now, on the porch, I was having the same feelings of wanting to escape before I got myself into a mess.

My employer pursed her lips in disapproval when she saw Cynthia standing on the steps with me, but she simply held the door open for both of us and informed us that we would spend the day working upstairs. I was to clean a couple of rooms up there, gather more laundry, and wait for her to negotiate the rent with a few tenants, "without trying to make them feel as if I am monopolizing their time." "Their sheets are in the dryer," she concluded, "let me get them out, and we can take them upstairs."

I whispered, "Oh God." I was reluctant to go upstairs with her, thinking it was probably a plot. I felt both glad and guilty that Cynthia had been softhearted enough to accompany me on this soon-to-become-momentous day. I couldn't believe that we were in this predicament. We didn't know the lady. She could take us upstairs and lock us in one of the bedrooms. As the old lady was grabbing the sheets from the dryer, Cindy whispered, "I can't believe you got me into this."

I replied, "I'm sorry. I'll make it up to you. I could pump gas for your dad one Saturday."

She looked at me and said jokingly, "My father would never let you work at his station. You'd scare away all of the customers. You'd probably fill their tanks up with the wrong gas." I was hurt by this remark, but still glad that she was with me as we headed upstairs.

The old lady, sheets in hands, said, "Follow me. We have to go out the front door. There is an entrance behind the gate on the side of the house. I wanted my renters to be able to come and go as they please."

I felt like crying. All I could think was, "Why aren't we off shopping?" I thought about the car I was saving for, and my worries lessened. Cynthia shut the front door behind her as the old lady directed her to do. The lady walked down the sidewalk, making an abrupt left near her garage. Cynthia and I followed her every move, not wanting to get reprimanded. I didn't know what to expect, and feelings of fear were overtaking me again because I was prone to anxiety attacks over my shy nature and experiencing new things. Part of this stemmed from my sheltered upbringing. Being sheltered meant that I never had to experience too much change. What was I going to find at the top of the stairs? What type of person would be renting a room from such an authoritative lady?

The old lady looked at me. "You're tall. Can you reach your hand over the fence and grab the latch?"

I did just as I was told, a bit fearful of what I was getting involved in. I thought about calling the employment agency and complaining about the duties that the old lady had us do. She was putting us in danger. We weren't told that we would be cleaning a stranger's living quarters. The job description had changed. We were no longer cleaning crystal and shining silver. We would be making beds and vacuuming. I would certainly make a phone call when I got home.

The old lady took a set of keys out of her pocket and said, "I called Margaret earlier to let her know that we were going to be bringing her clean sheets." The lady opened the door and we followed her into a tiny room that was barely big enough to fit three people. The stairwell was adjacent to the door. We followed the old lady up the stairs. I glanced back at Cynthia to see how she was handling the suspense. She rolled her eyes at me. I could understand her emotions, because I was feeling irritated at wanting to get this experience over with, too. The old lady stopped at the top of the stairs and knocked lightly on a door to her right. A middle-aged woman answered a couple of minutes later and said, "Hello. Come in."

The old lady said, "No, we just wanted to drop off your sheets."

The assumed renter looked at us, introducing herself as Margaret. Margaret took the sheets and told the lady, "I have a leaky faucet. Do you mind coming in and taking a look?"

The old lady looked back and told us, "You two stay right here. I'll be right back. Don't move." Margaret took the old lady in to show her the sink, leaving the door open. I had full view of the large living area and figured that the old lady would be not only looking at the leaky faucet, but negotiating the rent as planned. I became a bit self-conscious when I looked over to the far wall and saw a tall boy lying on a daybed. He was dressed only in shorts, his long legs hanging over the bed. He glanced up at us and said, "Hi." He didn't bother getting up to introduce himself like his mom had. He was looking over pamphlets with the word "University" splashed across the front.

For just a moment our eyes locked. I felt an instant chemistry brewing between us. I had never seen such a gorgeous boy in my life. I liked the way his straight blond hair, being a bit on the long side, was swept across his forehead. His blue eyes were irresistible; so were his nose, cheeks, and lips, from what I could see behind the pamphlets. Black eyebrows accented his sea blue eyes, making them sparkle in the sunlight that was filtering through the room. I noticed how long his body was and wondered if he played basketball. He was obviously still in high school, because he was looking at university pamphlets. He could also be a surfer, tanned and blond, possibly spending long hours at the beach. I remembered the old lady telling us that the renters just moved here from Rochester, New York. I didn't think people in Rochester did much surfing. The boy didn't seem insecure, but had a sense of self-assuredness about him. He seemed to know that his future would entail going off to college, furthering his education. I wasn't used to seeing boys who had goals and aspirations. The boys I knew only had aspirations to surf and party, thoughts of college not even on their agenda.

The boy didn't say much. He seemed to be content lying on the daybed, reading college materials. The moment was short lived: the lady came back to the door a couple minutes later. The feelings I had when the door closed were far from innocent. My fear and curiosity turned to arousal and desire, an internal force that felt both invigorating and alien.

I had to come up with a plan to get to know this boy, this ethereal influence who had brought me into such a state of euphoria. Who cared about the etiquette of place settings, music, and intimate occasions? If there was such a thing as "love at first sight," I knew that I had just experienced it. Little did I realize when we left the house that day, that my friend and co-worker felt the same way. I didn't think she'd even gotten a glance of the boy, because I was standing in front of her. We drove home in silence, an unusual occurrence in the silver caddy, daydreaming as the far away parental influence spoke, "What happened to you two today? Why're you so quiet?"

Who could resist?

CHAPTER FOUR
EXTEMPORANEOUS

The first thing I did when I got home that day was look at the beautiful dress that had come to represent my romantic dreams and ambitions. I wondered if maybe I liked the boy—the landlady said his name was Bill—because he was different. Rochester, New York, seemed excitingly far away. I wanted the experience of having a boyfriend, and I felt that fate had led me to Bill. The gray-haired old lady explained that her renters moved to Ventura so that Margaret, a single mother, could be closer to her parents in Ojai. "Where is Bill's father?" I wondered. Margaret, Bill's mother, worked as a nurse at an alcoholic rehabilitation facility in the area.

I thought about the upcoming "Backwards Dance," an event that would be taking place at my school the next month. I would ask Bill—after all, that's what the dance was all about, girls asking boys to attend. I had new determination, a goal in life that I knew I could accomplish. The only problem was that the old lady no longer needed me to work at her home. She had only needed me to help prepare for her upcoming party. How was I going to get past her and ask Bill to the dance? I thought about calling the old lady's home and asking for Bill's phone number, but I only met Bill once, and a phone call would be awkward. I needed some type of strategy in order to ask him out without seeming too presumptuous. But if I was going to ask him in person, how in the world would I get there? I didn't drive a car, but I did have a bike—and I knew that I had to act quickly if I wanted him as my date. I made a tentative plan: I would come home from school, ride my bike down to the old lady's home, and ask Bill to go with me. I thought to myself that I'd have to keep the whole experience a secret from my parents and friends.

I could hardly contain my excitement the next day, saying a quick prayer during mass for God's intervention. I knew I was stubborn and determined enough; nothing would get in my way of asking Bill to the dance. My friends at school noticed the glow on my cheeks and the excitement in my body language as I sat in religion class, not hearing a word the instructor said. They sensed that something about my personality had changed over the weekend, which placed new tension in our relationship.

I made it through my classes without divulging my secret to friends. "I have to get to Bill before someone else does," I thought. My father picked me up in front of the school. Getting into the passenger side of the car, I asked him to take me home. Any other day, I'd have enjoyed having him drop me off at my mother's beauty shop, but today was special.

My dad seemed preoccupied, saying, "I need to pick up your brother first." The junior high school my brother attended was located across the street from the house Bill lived in.

I asked my dad, "Can't you drop me off at home first?" My parents were flexible enough with their work schedules to accommodate us most of the time.

My dad said, "No, I need to get you both home so I can get back to the office. I'm meeting clients at five. I'll be home after I show them property."

I replied, "Is Mom at the shop?"

My dad, who was about to make a U-turn in front of my school, said, "Your Mother called. She'll be home by six."

I had a couple of hours before my parents would be home. "They'll never find out," I thought to myself as I looked at the beautiful green hills above my school. Within the hour, I'd get to see the boy whose gorgeous blue eyes had stared back at me and glinted in the sunlight filtering through his living room yesterday.

Nob Hill is the name of my street. The last time I rode my bike down the steep hill, where abundant green ivy surrounded wealthy homes, was a couple years back. I hadn't ridden my bike since my neighbor, Trisha, lost her brakes and ended up steering her bike up a driveway that wasn't her own. Trisha and her bike did a flip, landing in a bed of ivy, unscathed. I wondered if I would emerge from my own ride unscathed. I wanted to have a tryst with a boy I only met once. I was having adult emotions, and I was only fifteen. "It was tormenting." I thought. Still, as I walked down the flight of steps to my garage, I felt immense determination to carry out my plan. I opened the garage door and walked over to my dusty bike.

Checking the brakes on my bike would be smart, I thought. My father kept our bikes in tip-top condition, but I didn't want to perform the same maneuver Trisha had. I wouldn't worry about flipping my bike, I decided. All I needed to worry about was my timing, giving myself an hour to complete my task before my parents would be home. Because the whole ride was downhill, I would be at the old lady's home in approximately ten minutes.

I hopped on the ten-speed bike and took off down the hill, hoping my brother would be able to keep himself occupied. I remembered my father's advice: "Try not to use your brakes too much when you go down the hill. Use them sporadically, so you don't burn them out."

I was glad that I'd had a chance to change out of my school uniform, a green and gold skirt. Wanting to wear regular clothes, but not look too made up, I opted for jeans and a T-shirt. Dressing up would have to be saved for the dance. Being tall and thin, I was blessed with a good figure. That wasn't always the case.

Having a good figure didn't come naturally. I spent my elementary years overweight, until my mother put me on the swim team. My mother's best friend since the third grade, Ida, put her own children on a swim team in Florida. When Ida called my mother and told her that her daughter Lori had won first place in the backstroke, my mother knew that she had to get her own kids to join a team so that she could obtain her own bragging rights.

My mother would pick us up from school and take us to the public swimming pool saying, "Don't whine about swimming tonight."

My brother and I would complain, "But Mom, the pool's so cold."

My mother would reply, "It's my law. You're swimming every night, so quit complaining."

When we pulled up to the pool's drop-off point, I would continue begging, "But Mom, I don't know how to dive! Remember the coach's daughter tried to show me?" When she dove in, she'd hit her head on the bottom of the pool.

My mother didn't care. We were swimming, and she drove off quickly so that she could get back to her beauty shop. She most likely had a client waiting, head in rollers underneath one of the many dryers in her successful salon. My mother would always return an hour after she dropped us off, asking, "How was practice tonight?" She would ask us as if she couldn't remember our discussion when she had dropped us off.

Swimming helped me burn calories. I swam until my lungs hurt, and I do admit that it gave me energy and the ability to eat whatever I wanted. It wasn't until I turned twelve that I was able to enjoy fitting into fashionable clothes. I grew five inches in seventh grade. I was twelve years old and had a model's body. I still did, three years later. I was tall and thin with a fat girl's mind, and I knew I could use my body to get Bill to go to the dance with me. But as the wind blew through my hair and I inched closer and closer to where I met Bill just the day before, I began to worry: what if he said no?

I had been rejected recently enough by three boys—Scott, Chris, and Tim. In seventh grade I attended an Episcopal school in mid-town Ventura. I'd had a schoolgirl crush on a boy named Scott. Scott had gotten wind that I was going to break up with him because of my own insecurities about having a crush. He called me one night to tell me, "I'm calling to break up with you." This break-up, especially since it was done over the phone and not in person, was my first real ego-crushing experience. I was devastated. I thought about the Dear John letter I received from another boy, Chris—a tall, blond-haired, blue-eyed water polo player four years older than me. I met Chris at the Ondulando Club, a members-only club located around the corner from my house. I like to frequent the club on weekends and long summer days, sun-worshiping in one of the chaise lounges surrounding the Olympic pool. Chris noticed in his letter that he thought I was older than I was. He thought that I was of age to date, never imagining that I would be taking a chaperone to accompany us wherever we went. The thing is, my parents liked Chris and his all-American good-boy looks. They trusted him and were swayed when he asked them one night, "Can I take your daughter on a date?" My mother looked at him and said protectively, "You can, but her brother will have to accompany the two of you."

My first date with Chris was spent in the backseat of his car, kissing passionately. My brother sat in front, eating his large popcorn, Icee, and box of candy, all of which Chris used to bribe him. He'd made his conditions explicit, warning my brother that he would only buy the treats "if you promise not to say anything about what happens tonight to your parents." But my brother, not to be lured by a box of Jordan Almonds, told my parents that we didn't watch the movie because we were busy in the backseat. I was put on probation from dating until I turned sixteen.

The most recent rejection I experienced was when Tim dropped me off in front of my house, not even bothering to walk me to the door. Tim was upset that I spent the whole evening at his school dance talking to a classmate. Tim, a popular baseball player at Buena high school, didn't say a word as he sped to my house, ninety miles an hour on a windy two-lane road.

I didn't want to think about how I would feel if Bill declined my invitation to the dance, fearing that he attended the same school as Tim and Chris. It occurred to me, as I turned onto the street where he lived, that Bill might have been friends with both Chris and Tim.

I didn't have a problem riding my bike through the streets. I used all the biking signals my father had taught me. When I wanted to turn left, I placed my left arm out to warn the traffic behind me. Before I knew it, I was turning left on a flat, tree-lined street, the homes much more modest than my own.

I thought better of parking my bike in the old lady's driveway. I knew that she would most likely tell the employment agency if I was caught philandering with her tenants. I had no reason to be at her home. I hadn't forgotten anything, although I was going to use forgetfulness as an excuse if I needed one. I had spent the whole day planning. My backpack was crammed with various forms of makeup, including the Bonne Bell lip gloss that had been specially delivered to me after I'd ordered them from an ad in *Teen Magazine*. This lip gloss was special to me, and I took it with me everywhere. I received five different flavors, promising two of them to my best friend. My friend, Ally, was extremely disappointed when I broke my promise and decided to keep all five. Ally ended up writing a letter to the Bonne Bell company explaining how her friend had broken her promise, how she loved the product, was looking forward to using the gloss, and was quite distraught. Ally showed up at school a couple of weeks later, told me she'd received ten different flavors for free, and walked off without another word. I'd just experienced my first bout of payback, a painful thing women do to one another in response to being dissed, teased, or dumped as BFF'S.

I parked my bike, opening my backpack so I could retrieve my lip gloss, and said a quick prayer, "Please God, don't let the old lady come out of her house. If she does come out, please let me find a good excuse for my coming back." I was hoping that she had already picked up her mail. If she hadn't, I would be caught red-handed. I considered simply telling the truth: "I think I'm in love with your tenant's son, and I just came over to let him know I want him to be my boyfriend. I'm not going to let you stand in the way of my happiness."

I also envisioned a more desperate speech: "Get out of my way. I'm going up and you can't stop me. I'm in love with that boy. You can't threaten to keep me away. I'll do whatever I can to speak with Bill again." I decided, however, that I was taking desperate measures as it was. I rang the doorbell on the side gate, the same one that the lady had rung the day before, my hands shaking.

Bill opened the gate door a couple of minutes later, As if he'd known I was going to come over. I gave him a shy look, the tension in my neck mounting to new extremes. I had no time to think about the moment, about what I was going to say. I just blurted out, "Hi. I met you yesterday. Would you like to go with me to a dance at my school next month? It is called a Backwards Dance. The girls are supposed to ask the boys. I knew that you were new in town and thought that it would be nice if I could show you around ... I'm Pamela, by the way."

Bill looked at me, those black Italian eyebrows raised in curiosity. My pulse was racing beneath my skin. I was going to faint. Bill looked at me kindly and gave me an answer that I hadn't expected: "I'm Bill. I'd like to go to the dance with you. I'm glad you came back over. Why don't you give me your number? We can talk a little more over the phone. The landlady doesn't like people talking out here. She has so many rules it's like we're on probation."

I laughed, my heart skipping a couple of beats. Bill was actually talking to me. He wanted to get to know me better, too. The feelings I'd had earlier were justified. Every word out of his mouth seemed to be compassionate. Bill was gregarious, friendly. I looked up at him, noticing that he was much taller than I was. He was quite muscular, too. I asked him, curious as to why he was looking at the university pamphlets, "Are you in college?"

He replied with a chuckle, "No, not yet. I'm a senior at Buena."

Ventura, a small coastal town fifty miles north of Los Angeles, has three high schools. Buena is located in east Ventura. Their rival, Ventura High, is located about seven miles west of Buena. My high school was located between the two. I swam at the Buena pool and had been on the local swim team. I quit the team when I started ninth grade, high school. Since swimming as a sport was not offered at my high school, a Catholic college preparatory school, I had to give up the only sport I was good at. I was a good swimmer, especially in the breaststroke, but not as good as my brother, who had placed third in the county in the freestyle. I missed seeing the motivating words, "No Gain Without Pain," that were painted on the inside of the Buena high school's pool. I knew that the words would hold true in my everyday life, as well.

I was starting to feel comfortable with Bill, but I was still uncomfortable standing in the old lady's driveway. "I used to swim there," I told him. "I live up the hill. I go to private school, but I should be going to Buena. My neighbors go there, though."

Bill said, "I like going to school there, but it's different from my school in Rochester. We just moved here last month, so I don't really know a lot of people." He paused, looking back at the house. "Thanks for coming by. I'll call tonight to see if you made it up that hill in one piece." Bill walked me to my bike, where I fumbled trying to get back on the seat. He handed me my backpack, which I left by his gate. The backpack was so light that Bill commented, "There's nothing in here. Why're you carrying it?"

I looked at him, feeling a bit silly sitting on my bike, and said, "I wanted to bring it in case your landlord saw me talking to you. I was going to tell her I forgot something at her house."

Bill chuckled and stood there looking tall and lean, his legs tanned from wearing shorts in the California sun.

I wasn't surprised that I had enough energy to ride all the way home, crisscrossing back and forth up Nob Hill. I was ecstatic that our first real meeting went exactly as planned. I would relive the moment over and over in my mind when I got home, tucked away in the solitude of my bedroom. I would wait happily for Bill to call, thinking, "Bill said yes. He actually said yes."

CHAPTER FIVE
SADIE HAWKIN'S DANCE

Riding my bike up the hill as fast as I could, I got home before my parents did. I went straight to my bedroom after I closed the garage door, my muscles weak. Happy that my plans had gone so well, I couldn't get over how sweet Bill had been at our first real meeting. He was friendly, and much taller than I would have thought. I couldn't believe I asked him out on a date! How embarrassing! I really hadn't known how else to go about meeting him. He was more handsome than I had imagined, his eyes deep blue like the ocean. He looked as good in his T-shirt and shorts as he had when I first noticed him lying on the daybed. I wondered when he planned on calling me. Our first meeting had been so vague. I'd just introduced myself and asked him to the dance. I had a positive outlook on life and relationships, even though I didn't have that much experience. Then I thought about the Dear John letter. It had broken my heart. Chris's words stung me anew as I went to my closet and picked up the letter from the secret box I had tucked away so that nobody could find it. "Pamela, although I like you, I didn't realize how young you were. I don't know what I was thinking when I asked you out on a date."

I was not going to let my heartache keep me from asking Bill to the dance. When my parents finally arrived home, they noticed that I had a newly acquired glow on my face. I was excited about life, and they could see the change. My mother had already heard about Bill, because I told her when I got home the night before, but she didn't know that I asked him to the upcoming dance. I didn't know if I was going to tell my parents, but with the newly acquired glow and smile, they would surely ask why I was so happy. I was determined to go no matter what my parents said.

I ended up telling my mother and father that Monday night. I explained to them, suddenly overcome with emotion, "We're having a Sadie Hawkin's Dance at my school. I asked Bill." They were amazed, my father saying, "You don't even know this boy. How'd you find the nerve to ask him out on a date?"

My mother then told me that she wanted to meet Bill before the dance, saying, "Maybe we should have Bill over for dinner this weekend so we can meet him?"

I was happy that my parents were being open-minded about the date, and said, "Really! You'd do that for me?" They could see the determination in my eyes. My mother and father had given me the world while I was growing up. They threw elaborate parties for me, dressed me in nice clothes, and took me to Disneyland every year. They wanted the best for me and knew that I would probably put up a fight if they said no; trying to change their minds with each word I spoke. I was going to the dance with Bill.

My parents were excited for me, my dad saying, "I think I'll leave you two to the birds and bees conversation." With that, he got up and went into the kitchen to get a glass of water.

My mother told me about how she and Dad had met: they were on a triple date at Cerento beach, near Santa Monica. My mother was with a boy she considered to be just a friend; my father was with a girl named Glenna. My mother had had a crush on my father since she first saw him, giving a speech while he was running for student council. She went into the water to shake off some nervous energy and got caught in a riptide. My father saved her, and twenty-seven months later, they were married.

I secretly loved hearing stories about my parents' courtship, but I protested. "Mom, I'm just going to a dance. I'm not getting married!"

My mother looked at me and said, "You know I was a virgin when I got married. Your father and I dated two years and never had sex."

I rolled my eyes. "I'm not having sex, either. I am attending a dance with a boy who just moved here. He doesn't know many people and goes to Buena. I'm sure you'll like him. Please don't compare apples to oranges."

My mother came over, gave me a big hug, and said, "You're much more mature than I was at your age. I want you to experience life. I've always longed for more ... attention from your father ..." She trailed off, but I knew what she wasn't telling me. My mother wanted to feel loved, in a physical way. But my father was always so busy working, never spending as much time with us as a family. I thought their marriage was a good one, but it didn't seem to bring my mother the love, physical and mental, that she craved. This wasn't the first time I'd heard that my mother was a virgin when they got married. My mother continued. "I wore a hand-sewn, white dress down the aisle at my wedding, and I deserved it. The night of our honeymoon was ... difficult and painful."

I couldn't take any more sexual education from my mother. "Please stop," I asked plaintively, "I can't talk about this anymore. This is sick talking, about Dad like you don't love him."

My mother, a stubborn woman, kept right on talking, "I just don't want you to make the same mistakes I did."

I looked at her and said, "What do you mean? You want me to have sex before I get married?"

My mother looked down at the floor and whispered, "No. I want you to make the right decisions. I don't want you to base your decisions on my relationship with your father. Looked how my life has turned out. Your father is never home. He works too hard. I don't want you to be as naïve as I was when I got married. If that means that you have sex before you get married, then have sex. You'll be dating soon and I want you to make good decisions."

I was a busy teenager, and this conversation with my mother needed to get back on track. "Mom, let's quit talking about this. I need new accessories for my blue dress. I'm going to wear it to the dance. Can you take me to Broadway this weekend?" Broadway was a department store at the Ventura mall. My parents had given me a credit card there, so I could buy anything I wanted—within reason.

My mother glanced back up at me, sadness still in her eyes. "Yes, but we need to set aside some time to meet Bill. I'll let your father know that we'll have him for dinner next Saturday. We can go shopping on Sunday after church, because your father will most likely be holding an open house." It was my turn to hug my mother. I was excited that she was letting me go to the dance with Bill, even though she seemed sad, almost down. I would make it a point to speak with her when my father was out of earshot. I wondered to myself if they weren't getting along.

When the phone rang, I jumped up and ran to answer it.

Sure enough, it was Bill on the other end of the line, wondering if I had made it home okay. "I had my mother drive me up the hill after you left. Those hills are steeper than I thought. Foothill Road seems awfully dangerous—two lanes and not a sidewalk in sight."

I took the phone into my bedroom, giving my parents the signal for silence as I ran past them both, now seated on the living room couch. I sat on my bed, smiling as I spoke, "Yeah, I made it home in one piece. I ride fast on Foothill, usually against traffic so that people will see me."

Bill, who had a nice telephone voice, thanked me for asking him to the dance.

Wanting to be polite, I replied, "You must miss your friends back home?"

Bill said, "I do, but my mother has been wanting to move to California for a long time. She's talked about it for years. My grandparents are getting up there in age, so we decided that now was as good a time as any to move out west to be closer to them."

Remembering that his grandparents lived in Ojai, I said, "Why didn't you move to Ojai? It's quite a ways away from here."

Bill started laughing. "My mother wanted to live close, but not that close to them. She still wants her freedom to do as she pleases. We both fell in love with Ventura. I wanted to learn to surf. My mother knew that it would be more difficult for me to get to the beach if we lived in Ojai."

Wanting to keep the conversation light, I asked, "Do you surf?"

Bill replied, "I've taken my board out a couple of times."

I was impressed. "You have a board?

Bill, who was obviously was getting a kick out of my gullible personality, replied, "Of course I have a board. Doesn't everyone who lives here have a board?"

"I don't."

"If you want, I can take you to the point one of these days. You can watch me surf and let me know if I'm any good, or if I should pack it in and head back to New York."

"My brother surfs. He's at Point all the time. I'd like to watch you surf, but don't try to get me out in the water."

Bill seemed perplexed. "I thought you were a good swimmer?"

I said, "I am, but not in the ocean. My brother took me out on his surfboard once. He wanted to teach me to surf. He ended up taking me over to a bed of seaweed. I thought that we'd be eaten by a shark. I knew that there were sharks in the area, and when the seaweed wrapped around my legs, I thought I'd run into one. I screamed at my brother to take me back to shore. He told me I was being a baby and took me further out. I haven't been in the ocean since."

Bill laughed, "There's nothing to worry about. Your chances of getting killed by a shark are slim."

"Well, I don't ever want to find out."

Bill replied, "What do you like to do besides swimming in pools, then?"

"I like to lie by the pool and soak up the sun."

We were both laughing when I heard a knock on my door. My mother looked in and said, "Dinner's almost ready. Wrap it up. Your father needs the phone."

I whispered, "Okay, Mom, I'll be right there."

Bill, hearing the whisper said, "What?"

I said, "Oh, my mother told me we're having dinner and my father needs to use the phone. Can you call me back later?" We hung up, and I lay back on my bed wondering if he thought I was immature because my parents wouldn't let me talk very long on the phone.

Bill did call me back later, and I explained to him that my parents wanted to meet him. He agreed to come to my house for dinner. Bill didn't seem nervous, but sincere and sweet. I hung up the phone knowing that I had made the right decision in asking him out. I went to sleep that night hoping that someday Bill would be my boyfriend. He brought excitement into my life. I stared up at the stars shining out my huge bedroom windows. Life was good. I was fifteen and on the verge of my first experience being in love.

When Bill arrived that next Saturday I was amazed at how polite and well-spoken he was with my parents. His table manners were sophisticated, polished like the silver of our place settings. We had a great dinner. My parents seemed to enjoy Bill's company. They even let him sit at the head of the table, opposite my father. It seemed that my mother and Bill were able to understand each other on a more emotional level. My mother seemed most interested in Bill's road trip to Ventura, asking him questions like, "How long did it take you to drive to Ventura from Rochester?"

"It took us two weeks," Bill said. "We stopped and did some sightseeing along the way."

Liking the fact that Bill seemed to enjoy traveling, my mother asked, "What places did you like the best?"

Not knowing that he was about to answer a loaded question, Bill said, "I enjoyed every stop we made. Just spending time with my mother made the road trip more fun."

My mother, being extremely chatty that night, said, "Did you go to Washington DC?"

Bill said, "As a matter of fact, we did. I really enjoyed sightseeing there. We walked all around the Capital building, the National Monument, and the White House. Mom and I stayed in motels along the way. I liked Washington DC, but I'd been there many times before. We only stayed a day, because we were both pretty anxious to get to California."

My mother replied, "Did Pamela tell you that I took her to Washington DC once? I drove our motor home around the United States with my children and their grandmother, Alice. I remember pulling into Washington DC at night. I found an empty parking lot on the Potomac River. I parked and got up into my bunk. The kids and my mother were fast asleep in their own beds. At around two in the morning, I heard talking outside the motor home door. At first I thought it was the police, wanting me to leave and find a KOA to park the motor home. All of a sudden, the motor home started shaking. If it wasn't for my mother's snoring we could have been killed. To this day, I think that the gang of boys thought there was a man inside. My mother saved us. I was stupid to put the kids in such danger. Thank God they didn't wake up! I don't think I've ever been so scared in my life! Did you ever have any experiences like that? I could go on and on ... how long do you have?"

I didn't know if my mother was trying to embarrass me or run Bill off; stories of my past seemed bound to surface somewhere in the dinner conversation. My dad and I stayed silent, wondering what stories my mother would come up with next. I did enjoy hearing about Bill's trip to Ventura, however.

Bill, wanting to include everyone at the table in the conversation asked, "Ryan, did you go on the trip with them?"

My father looked at Bill and said, "I met them in Minnesota after they came down through Michigan. I flew in to Minneapolis/St. Paul, where Pat picked me up. We ended up staying at a local KOA, because I could only stay two days. I had to get back to work."

My mother started laughing and didn't let my father finish telling his story, saying, "When Ryan arrived, the first thing I had him do was to empty the sewage from the motor home. It hadn't been emptied since we left Ventura. Boy, was he upset when the valve broke. Sewage spilled all over him. He went to take a shower, but you had to pay fifty cents. He came running back, furious with me. I'll never forget the look on his face as he was running back from the men's restroom begging me to give him two quarters."

My father said, "I was so happy to get back on the plane and come home to Ventura. I don't know how Pat managed the motor home, two kids, and her mother on the trip. She wanted to take her mother around the country because Pat knew that her mother, Alice, wouldn't be around much longer."

It was my turn to speak up and tell what happened next, "Grandma looked at me one day and asked for a toothpick, but was pointing at the paper towels. I told Mom to stop the motor home, that something was wrong with Grandma."

My mother, who was getting quite emotional, said, "My mother had a mini stroke in Kentucky. I think the trip may have been too much for her, especially with all of the excitement we had along the way. I had to put her on a plane and fly her back to Arizona to be with my older sister while we finished the trip. She died a year later. I think the whole experience affected Pamela the most. She was extremely close to my mother. I'm glad that she got to see the beauty of America and Canada before she died."

Bill must have felt the sadness in the air, and he tried desperately to change the subject, saying, "You said your mother flew back to Arizona—is that where you're from?"

Pat said, "I was born in Pacoima, down by Los Angeles. I was the last of seven children. My father was a contractor. He and Mom homesteaded in Florence, Arizona. Since he was a contractor and homes weren't being built like they are now in Arizona, we went back and forth from Arizona to California all my life." My mother cut her food into smaller pieces and continued speaking, "I did go to second grade at Florence Elementary. I met my best friend, Ida there. Her family owns farmland in Florence. I had the best time that year, riding horses, exploring the desert, and hiking. When my mother died, I was the only one out of seven children who could afford to purchase the homestead. It holds more sentimental value than anything. My brother lives across the street from the homestead. He's a contractor just like my father was."

Bill said, "Pamela says you own a beauty salon in Ventura? Do you cut men's hair?"

My mother, who loved elaborating, said, "Yes. It's on Main Street. It's called The Hairbenders. Come by sometime and I'll give you a haircut, although I carry my scissors with me wherever I go. If you want, I'll be glad to give you a haircut now."

Bill laughed. "I'd prefer to come into the shop, if that's okay."

My mother looked at Bill. She always sat at the part of the table with the best view of the city lights below. She seemed happy to be seated next to Bill, the two of them carrying on a conversation while I looked dreamily into his blue eyes. They seemed to sparkle with each flicker of the candles, and a bolt of electricity ran the length of my body each time he glanced over at me.

Surely Bill was having a good time. The more my parents learned about him, the more they seemed to relax. Bill offered to clear the table when the meal was complete. I heard him talking to my mother while they loaded the dishwasher, my mother's voice saying, "Did I hear you say your mother's a nurse? I've always wanted to be a nurse. Does she work at one of the local hospitals?"

Bill replied, "She works at an alcohol treatment facility in Oxnard. She seems to enjoy her job, but I worry about the type of people that she comes into contact with."

Thinking better of leaving them alone together, not knowing where the conversation might lead, I walked into the kitchen and said, "Mom, why don't you go watch TV with Dad? I'll do the dishes."

They both looked at me. Bill smiled, but resumed his duty as dishwasher loader. I thought about the trip my mother had bravely taken us on before my grandmother died. I remembered going to New York, was glad that I would have something in common with Bill. My favorite place in New York, besides New York City, was Niagara Falls. I was fascinated by the dangerous aspect of the falls, listening intently as the tour guide told us about the brave souls who had tried to travel down the falls in wooden barrels—often to perish. I wondered what kind of mental state one would have to be in to attempt such a dangerous feat. The area near the falls also seemed very romantic to me, and I watched honeymoon couples enjoying the hot springs with interest. I resolved to return to New York someday—maybe for my own honeymoon. I couldn't believe I'd met someone from the part of the world that so fascinated me. I thought about the journal entries I'd made after we left New York. I made it a point to open the journal that night to reread my entries: "Niagara is very romantic. I saw couples kissing in the hot springs. They must be on their honeymoon. This seems like a passionate place. I intend to return with my own husband someday."

A couple weeks later when we arrived to the dance, Bill who suggested we get in line to take a photo together. He was dressed in Levi blue jeans and a nice, light blue cotton shirt. His blond hair was combed neatly to the side, freshly trimmed by my mother. My heart skipped a few beats when he suggested that we get our picture taken together. I thought back to the past several days, my anticipation about the dance keeping me up most nights. My parents seemed to like Bill. After he'd left that first Saturday, my mother had said simply, "He seems like a nice boy. You'll have a great time with him at the dance." I remembered looking at them in happy shock. They had given me the go-ahead, even though they had remained firm in the past: I had to be sixteen to date. Bill and I had spoken on the phone every single night after he came over for dinner. He had his driver's license, so my parents didn't have to drop us off. I was amazed—and gratified—that my parents let me go with him. It was as if they trusted Bill to take care of me even though they had only interacted with him a couple of times.

When the pictures were developed and distributed a couple of weeks after the dance, all I could do was look at them. Bill and I were standing against a photo backdrop of blue sky and white clouds. We were standing beneath an arch of white flowers and green leaves. Bill had his arm wrapped around my waist. I wasn't standing close to him, because I was nervous. Our outfits complimented each other. I wore the pretty Jessica McClintock dress I had modeled, which was navy blue with little pink flowers and long, sheer white, puffed sleeves. Bill had a serious look on his face, his lips slightly turned up at the sides, no pearly white teeth showing. I was smiling ear to ear, happy to have a photo of our first date. My hair was long and golden, combed in a layered Farrah Fawcett hairdo that was popular at that time. We looked as if we belonged together. When Bill asked me to slow dance after our photo session, my heart melted. I was feeling many new emotions. I was shy, scared, and open to the many possibilities that our future together held.

Cynthia came up to me that night and said, "I'm mad at you. I was going to ask Bill to the Backwards Dance."

I winked at her and said, "I thought you might, so I asked him the day after we met him. I think I'm in love."

Every one of my friends commented on how cute Bill was. They all asked me where I'd met him, what school he attended, and where he was from. I told each of my inquiring friends, "I'll tell you the whole story later, when he's not around."

Bill took me home that night, walked me up to the front door, and gently kissed me on my lips. I melted in his arms, my knees weak. I was not equipped, mentally or physically, for the strong rush of emotions I was feeling. I knew I could no longer disguise my emotions, which were quite overwhelming. I wanted more, but knew that the proper thing to do was to politely say, "Thanks for going to the dance tonight. You've caused quite a stir at my school. Everyone is wondering where I met you.... I had a great time."

Bill whispered into my ear, "So did I. Make sure you only say good things about me."

I looked into his eyes, feeling the warmth of my red face, trying to flirt back. "Don't worry, I won't say anything but good things about you."

Not long after I walked into my bedroom that night, there was a knock at my door. My mother opened the door a crack, saying, "Pamela, Bill's on the phone."

I picked up the phone. "Bill?"

He replied, "I just wanted to say good night. I had a great time tonight."

"Me too. Did you get home safely? I was just thinking of how much my parents like you. You made quite an impression tonight."

"I like your parents, too. They're nice, not snobbish like most people who live on the hill."

I laughed, "People are nice up here."

Bill's voice was apologetic. "That's not what I meant! Some people with money can be conceited. That's one reason why we moved out here."

"Sorry about having to hear about our trip. I'm sick of hearing about it."

"I like road trips. Maybe we can take one someday."

I blushed. "That would be nice, but I don't think my parents would let me, although I'd love to go with you to Rochester. I want to see the place where you grew up."

Bill said sleepily, "It's a nice place."

I replied, not wanting to hang up, "Good night!"

"Good night! Sweet dreams."

After hanging up with Bill, I took the phone back into the kitchen. Placing it back into the cradle, I noticed my parents were deep in discussion.

My mother glanced up and said, "Pamela, come sit down."

I said, "What happened?"

My father said, "Nothing. We just want to speak with you for a minute."

I groaned, sitting at the same dining table where the introductory dinner had taken place saying, "What's up?"

My brother appeared in the room. "Poor Pammy, getting into trouble over a boy."

I looked at him and stuck out my tongue, hating having everyone's attention, "Johnny, get out of here."

My mother was the first to speak, "Pamela. I see a glow on your face. We just want to make sure you know what you're getting yourself into."

I replied, "I thought you guys liked Bill!"

My mother sounded almost threatening, "We want you to take this relationship slow."

"What do you mean slow?"

My father spoke up, "We see how you look at him. We're concerned that you might get hurt."

I replied, "Why are you so worried about my getting hurt now? Don't you have money to make and customers to please? It's a little late to be so concerned about me."

My father said, "Pamela, we wouldn't live in such a nice home if we didn't work. You wouldn't be going to private schools. We don't mean to be threatening. We just want you to take your relationship with Bill slow."

I tried to remain sweet as I indulged them in their attempt at influencing my life. I found my parents concern insulting. My parents, suspicions seemed to dissipate as I became more infuriated. They had never been this concerned about me. I walked back to my room, happy that my attempts to justify my friendship with Bill seemed to ease their suspicions. Although I didn't tell them, I wanted Bill, the boy who had walked into our home longing for the family he'd never had, to be the person to whom I surrendered my heart and soul. With each word spoken, each breath breathed, and each look given, Bill was gregarious and composed. He left me that night wanting more. My parents and I had a feeling that change was inevitable, my heart captured. I would never be the same, was open to emotional and spiritual growth. My life had taken on a new direction and my hardworking parents were trying to encroach on my bliss.

CHAPTER SIX
CHRISTMAS DAY 1979

Bill invited me to his aunt's house for a Christmas Day celebration with his family. I had already met his mother, Margaret. I wasn't sixteen yet, so we couldn't become an official couple, but Bill wanted to introduce me to his family. I savored the attention as he drove. Along the way I said, "No wonder you wanted to move here. I didn't know that your aunt lives here, too."

Margaret replied, "Yes. My family lives in California. They've begged me for years to move here. My sister's a school teacher for the Santa Barbara school district. Wait till you see her home. It's so cute. I hope that we find one like it someday."

Bill glanced at his mother, who was comfortably seated in the backseat and said, "I hope we find a house like it soon. That old lady is driving me crazy wanting me to fix this and help with that. She has me doing all of her chores."

I laughed. "No wonder the agency hasn't called me to come back. She's found a part-time employee. Has she had you shine her silver, yet?"

I heard Margaret chuckling in the background, but Bill didn't like talking about the old lady. Let's talk about something else. I think we're going to move into our own apartment after I graduate in June. Right, Mom?" Bill looked into the rear-view mirror, smiling at his mother.

I was happy at the prospect of Bill moving to an apartment. I was uncomfortable going to the old lady's home to see him. Bill and I had grown close after the dance. We talked every night on the phone. He came over weekly for dinner. I'd learned earlier that Bill's father left when Bill was two years old. Margaret was heartbroken over having to raise him without a father. Bill gave me pictures of himself as a rambunctious two-year-old. One picture was of him playing in a clothes hamper, the other of him seated on a tractor. When I looked at those pictures, I wondered how any father could leave a child as adorable as Bill.

Bill seemed to trust me, divulging information that affected him deeply. He told me during one of our nighttime phone calls that his mother had a drinking problem. "She's an alcoholic," he said quietly. I tried to take the information in stride, not knowing how to handle such a grown-up topic of conversation. My own parents drank alcohol, but I didn't think they were alcoholics. Sometimes, though, when my father would walk through the door after a long day at the office and pour himself a drink, my mother would get angry. "How dare you drink in front of the children?" She would ask in disgust. My father almost never had more than one or two drinks, but when he did, my mother would become enraged. One time my mother and father had a serious argument over his drinking. My mother ended up chasing my father through the house with a fire poker.

My mother, being the youngest of seven children, was quite spoiled. She grew up knowing that she was the most special person on the earth, but she was also a hard worker. She had worked hard for our family, owning her own business. We had a nice home, cars, and clothes, and my brother and I attended the best schools. When Bill told me about his mother, I knew that we shared something in common. My parents were probably alcoholics, too. They were dysfunctional. I understood where Bill was coming from, his own familial dysfunction apparent. He loved his mother and was protective of her, not wanting her to drink. Bill was less like son than a guardian angel who watched over his mother on a daily basis.

When Bill invited me to his aunt's for Christmas, I couldn't think of a better place to be. Bill even asked my mother and father one night as we were eating dinner, and I jumped up and said, "Can I go, please?"

My mother later sat me down and spelled out her worries. "You and Bill seem to be getting closer. Now, I like Bill, and so does your father. And we want you to know that we love you. But we're a bit concerned that you're moving too fast with this. Can't you two just be friends until you turn sixteen?"

I started crying. "Mom, I love Bill. He seems to feel the same about me. I want to meet the rest of his family. It's not like he's a stranger. He has family here. He's friends with our neighbors. They go to the same school. You don't have to worry. He has roots here, even though he and his mother just moved from New York."

One hurdle that I didn't mention that night at the dinner table was the fact that Bill and I were progressing quickly in our physical relationship, something my parents would be against. Bill had asked me, shortly after the dance, to bike over to his place after school.

I replied, "Of course." I figured that Bill wanted me to meet his mother on a more formal basis. When I arrived, secretly parking my bike inside the fence and hoping the old lady wouldn't see me as I knocked on his door, Bill was waiting.

Bill took me in his arms and said, "Hi. I missed you today. All I could think about was you, even though I had mid-terms."

I kissed Bill's cheek, feeling a bit embarrassed for having such immense feelings for him. "I bet you did great on the exams. You're so intelligent.... Which colleges are you going to apply to?"

This was a question I afraid to have him answer. When Bill replied, "I'd like to go back to New York, maybe the University of Rochester," it was as if he could feel my heart breaking. He quickly added, "There are some great universities here, too. I'll have to see where I get accepted. I'd like to stay close to my mother, so maybe I'll apply to UCSB."

I couldn't bear it if Bill moved to New York, so I tried to dissuade him. "I've always wanted to go to UCSB. I hear it's the best university. It's close to your aunt's home. You could probably live there while you go to school." What would that mean for our relationship? I had two years left of high school. I hadn't even thought about my own future. I figured that I would either attend college or get married. The future never entered my mind, especially since thoughts of Bill had consumed me.

I had attended many Christian schools in my short life. I went to church every Sunday. My father taught Sunday school. Would God approve of me meeting a person who would entice me into premarital sex? Would he banish me from the golden gates of Heaven? I had a moral dilemma. I wanted to get intimate with Bill, but I knew I was too young, as well as unmarried. When Bill escorted me up the stairs, taking me to a bedroom he had broken into, I had no will to resist. I lay on the bed as Bill artfully undressed me. I was oblivious to the world, only wanting more of what Bill was about to offer me. He moved with precision. I was fully aware of the fact that I was being seduced, thoughts of college long forgotten. Bill was gentle. I desired him more than I ever imagined I would desire another human being. He seemed surprisingly skillful and confident for a mere senior in high school. This left me wondering if there had been many others. I was too weak to speak. His sexual appetite appeared necessary to his being alive. My only worry, besides getting pregnant, was what I was going to tell my friends. Surely they would notice I had changed, become more mature. What would they think of me? I pictured them listening intently to my story while we were all seated on a school bench located in the sophomore quad. Since the dance, they couldn't get enough of my stories about Bill. They had never been confronted with such moral dilemmas because their parents were much more protective of them. My parents were more concerned about making money to support our lifestyle. What would I tell them about my first encounter with Bill?

As we were driving along the ocean highway to his aunt's home, I thought back to the stories I had told my friends about Bill, who picked me up that morning after he and his mother had shared an intimate Christmas morning opening their presents. My thoughts went to concern for what my parents would think about me if they knew that I had lost my virginity to Bill. Surely they didn't suspect that we were intimate in our relationship, because my mother would've been quite angry with me. As we opened our own Christmas presents that morning, my mother had said, "You should have invited Bill's family here for Christmas dinner. You know how much I enjoy cooking for people. Why don't you call him and ask him if they'd like to come here? I could put some extra plates on the table." I knew they didn't suspect a thing. They would never insist that Bill's family come to our home for Christmas if they suspected their daughter was living a sinful life.

I explained to my mother, as I was applying mascara to my straight eyelashes, trying to get ready for Christmas with Bill's family, "I'm looking forward to meeting Bill's family. His aunt doesn't have any kids. She isn't married. I think his family feels obligated to spend the holiday with her. Besides, this is the first Christmas Bill has lived here. And I couldn't cancel at the last minute." I didn't tell her that Bill's mother had drunk too much at a Christmas party the night before. He was upset, and I wanted to be there if he needed a shoulder to cry on. "I don't want to delegate where he'll have Christmas dinner," I continued. "I'll be home early. Maybe we can have our dessert when I get back home?" I wanted my mother to understand. My parents had given me a little leeway when it came to dating Bill. They had no choice. I would go to the ends of the earth for him, no matter what they said.

I enjoyed looking at the Polaroid picture that Bill's aunt had taken of us that Christmas Day. Bill's family was seated on a sectional couch that surrounded a glass coffee table, enjoying the fact that they were finally together. Bill and I were seated on the floor, sitting close to each other. I was dressed in red velvet pants, a white T-shirt, and a red sweater. Bill had made comments about how great I looked my hair in long golden long curls. Bill looked dashing as I tried hard to discourage his advancements. He wanted to cuddle and hold me, but I felt uncomfortable showing such emotion in front of his family. Deep down, a storm was brewing, and I couldn't wait until we were alone.

His grandparents were extremely friendly. His grandmother asked me, "Bill says you go to a Catholic school in Ventura. Are you Catholic?"

I smiled. Bill was tickling me, trying to make me laugh. I replied, "No. I'm not Catholic. My family attends a Christian church near our house. I went to eighth grade there. I met a couple friends who were going to attend the Catholic high school. I didn't like the thought of attending high school without them, so I begged my mom and dad to let me go there, too. Their mom drives us to school almost every day."

Bill said, "Pamela won't be needing a ride after she gets her license this June. She's going to get her permit soon." Bill had been teaching me to drive in my mother's Porsche. It had a stick shift, so I was having a difficult time learning to drive. I stalled the car at every stop sign. Once, at a stop sign on top of a hill, he had had to put the emergency brake on and trade seats with me. "We would've never made it home before her parents if I didn't do that," he told his family.

"Bill! Don't tell them that. It's hard to drive with a stick shift."

Seeing that I was getting embarrassed, Bill's grandmother said, "What do your parents do for a living?"

I replied, feeling like the spotlight was again on me, "My mother owns a beauty shop in Ventura. My dad sells real estate."

Margaret added, "Pamela's parents invited us over for dessert when we get back to Ventura. They have a beautiful home up on the hill. The view of the city from the balcony is spectacular."

Bill's family seemed genuine, nice. They seemed to care about me as a person, even though they did like the fact that I came from an upper-class family. I desperately wanted to get the spotlight off of me and was happy when the subject changed to how Margaret and Bill were adapting after their cross-country move.

Margaret's sister said, "How do you like living in Ventura?"

Margaret said, "I missed the autumn leaves this year. The fall colors and autumn harvests, picking out pumpkins, and hot apple cider in October … I miss those times"

Bill, feeling self-conscious that the topic of his childhood could possibly be discussed said, "Mom, you make it sound like I'm still a kid who likes to pick out pumpkins during Halloween."

Margaret laughed. "Honey, you love to pick out pumpkins in the fall. That was one of your favorite things to do. I like picking pumpkins, too. Adults enjoy spending time with family in the pumpkin patch. I was telling your aunt that we both miss that time of year. Rochester is a beautiful place in the autumn. They don't have the color out here like they do back home."

Bill, who liked his new home, said, "There's the ocean! I love living near the ocean—learning to surf has been as challenging as playing hockey or skiing."

Wanting to be included in the conversation and learn more about Rochester I said, "I bet you miss Rochester, though."

Bill said, "Mom just misses living on the lake. She liked going to the farmer's market on Saturday mornings, taking me to the Seneca Park zoo to see the African elephants, going to Broadway plays and musicals. Did you know that Rochester is called 'The Flower City?' It's a historical place. Susan B Anthony was arrested there in 1872 because she tried to vote, wanting to free the slaves. Her home is a historical landmark. Kodak invented the camera and film in Rochester, too. There's even a museum of photography that is internationally famous. I miss going to those places." Bill really seemed to be giving us enough information about his home town. He seemed to miss the area.

Learning about the city Bill recently lived in lifted my spirits. I hoped that he liked Ventura as much. I would hate to have Bill and his mother move back because they missed the fall leaves, the farmer's market, and the historical aspect of Rochester. I said, "Did you say that Rochester is near a lake?"

Margaret was the first to speak, melancholy filling the air, "Rochester borders Lake Ontario, the Erie Canal, and the Genesee River. We used to take river cruises on weekends. That's what I miss most—the biking, boating, and skiing. Bill loved to ski ... of course, I'm enjoying the weather in Ventura. It's about twenty degrees in Rochester as we speak."

With talk of the weather, the mood became cheery again. Bill's grandmother said, "Let's eat. Bill, will you open a bottle of champagne for us? The bottle happens to be one that you and your mom brought back from one of those wineries on Lake Ontario. Let's have a toast to you and Margaret moving here and our first Christmas together in a long time."

Bill said, "Let's toast to my meeting Pamela."

I smiled back at him as I heard the family say, "Yes. Let's toast to you meeting such a nice girl."

The day was spectacular, and I enjoyed learning so much about Rochester. Out of the blue, Bill mentioned to me on the way home, "I'm going to buy a Jeep after I get a job. I want to take you four-wheeling someday. There's a great place in the Santa Barbara Mountains." I noticed that Bill's eyes were filled with excitement when he talked about four-wheeling. I was amazed at his *joie de vivre*. I later learned that he enjoyed taking life to extremes, testing fate. I was more conservative, especially when it came to dangerous excitement. Bill's personality was the opposite of mine, and I became frightened with his talk about four-wheeling down a mountain. His every breath would be spent devouring and savoring all that life had to offer. He spent his time in fulfilling the dangerous, extreme aspect of his personality. I felt a large component of his life was spent trying to mask the emotional turmoil of his childhood. These legacies of his troubled childhood, his absent father and alcoholic mother, would add to his captivating personality in ways that most people would describe as foolish and dangerous. Nonetheless, I would go four-wheeling with Bill if that was what it took for him to fall in love with the area and not to move back to Rochester, the Flower City.

Bill was a humorous child

Bill at a farm in Rochester, NY

CHAPTER SEVEN
BUENA HIGH SCHOOL, CLASS OF 1980

Bill attended his graduation ceremony in June, 1980. He was determined to walk across the stage even though his mother wasn't present. His mother had disappointed him once again on this glorious day, and the familiar sadness filled his heart. I was amazed at Bill's ability to detach himself from the familiar situation, one that happened with such regularity in his life. I was proud that he could rise above his displeasure, still loving his mother as he accepted his diploma. I watched excitedly from a crowd of well-wishers who included his supportive grandparents.

Not being able to put up with her rules, Bill and his mother had moved out of the old lady's home a month before he graduated. They now lived in an apartment located behind the grocery store where we bought our food. Bill never told me if the old lady had had any knowledge of our tryst. He said, "My mother and I disagreed with all the old lady's rules. We moved in with her when we first moved here. We didn't know anybody, and the lady seemed nice at the time. My mother spent all our money getting us out here and didn't have a job. We took what we could get. We saw an ad in the paper, 'A room for rent,' and took it. She didn't require a deposit—probably was desperate as we were. I doubt she knew about us unless she was standing outside the door, listening."

I looked at him intently, saying, "Why didn't you move to Ojai with your grandparents? They seem nice. They could have helped you while you two found a place."

Bill replied, "My mother would never allow her parents to help us. If we moved to their home, she would constantly be watched. Knowing she has a drinking problem, they would never lose sight of the fact. An alcoholic finds ways to drink. It would never work if we lived with them."

Bill came to pick me up the day of his graduation. I had only been to one other graduation. I was finishing my freshman year and a couple of guys I knew were in the graduating class. Johnny Cash's daughter was also graduating, and I was excited to see the Man In Black. I spent the night staring at Johnny Cash, oblivious to the students getting their diplomas. He was seated on the bleachers, and I was amazed that people were respecting his privacy. The crowd had had four years of knowing that Johnny Cash's daughter went to the school, so having him seated in the bleachers was old hat to them by then. The students and their parents had most likely received his autograph at other school functions. Since I was just finishing my freshman year, though, all I could say—in a mesmerized tone—was, "Look, there's Johnny Cash!"

The only graduation that mattered this year would be Bill's. Most likely there weren't going to be any big celebrities in attendance. Bill picked me up on his new motorcycle, not yet able to afford a Jeep. He loved riding it because it gave him the freedom to explore and the release of adrenaline and endorphins he so craved. He rode the motorcycle at top speeds and sometimes he tried to pop wheelies. Since I was more cautious than he was, so I made sure that Bill didn't try any funny stuff while I was on the back of his bike. When I felt the energy he expelled while riding his motorcycle speeding up a bit, I would say, "Bill, slow down!"

Bill frowned, his jaw tightening, and said, "You never want to have any fun." It seemed like Bill wanted to take a gamble with our relationship that particular day. He wanted me to be happy, to be in a celebratory mood, but I was concerned he would crash his bike. He seemed to want to destroy the mood of the ceremony by taking his motorcycle to extremes. Bill was in a festive yet dark mood, entertaining me until we walked through the door of the apartment. His mother and her boyfriend were passed out in her upstairs bedroom.

Grad Night Knott's Berry Farm, 1980.

Bill made sure that I didn't come upstairs with him when he went to check on his mother. He had experienced this type of hurt many times in his life. His mother had disappointed him with her drinking binges in the past. He seemed to hold a grudge against anyone or anything that tempted his mother to drink. Rudy, a fellow alcoholic whom she had met at the treatment facility where she worked, was one of those people. He had tempted Margaret to drink with him before the ceremony. Bill said he had tried to stop them, but that "they must've had more when I went to pick you up." I was hurt that Bill was trying to place the blame on me. Margaret had made futile attempts in the past to stop drinking. Now, by dating Rudy, Margaret was taking a gamble with her own addiction. Bill told me the many stories about how Margaret would enthusiastically put her addiction to rest, only to succumb to the seduction of drink, inevitably falling off the wagon. I reflected, sadly, that I had recently disappointed him in a similar way.

I thought back to the time I had first experienced alcohol. I had been introduced to beer in my freshman year, long before I met Bill. Randy, a classmate, had asked me to dance with him. He had whispered in my ear, "I can get Mike's Mustang. Wanna go for a drive with me?"

I knew that if I left the dance, my parents would somehow find out. But a wild streak hidden under my shy veneer proved irresistible. I wanted to sneak away; after all I had known this particular classmate for a year. He seemed like a nice guy, was held in high regard by his classmates. What would it hurt if I went for a drive with him? His parents were successful, making their money from good ole Texas oil before his father was transferred out to work on the oil rigs off the California coast. I couldn't refuse when he continued whispering in my ear, "I promise to have you back in an hour."

I looked at him shyly and said, "All right. Let me tell my friends to cover for me, just in case my parents come to pick me up."

Randy took me down to Bonny Beach, a small stretch of beach where students from my school liked to hang out. He parked the borrowed Mustang near a sandy pathway. The moon was shining brightly overhead. He reached out and put his arm around me. Suddenly nervous, I said, "It's probably too cold to take a walk on the beach. We should head back. My parents might come early. They would kill me if they found out."

Grinning smugly, Randy said, "We'll go back. I promise. I want you to try something first."

I asked softly, "What?"

He chuckled, "I bought a six-pack before the dance. The liquor store owner didn't even card me."

I'd never had a beer before, didn't know what it tasted like. Before I could respond, Randy got out of the Mustang and went to the trunk to retrieve a six-pack of Coors Light. He shut the door quickly, taking his place behind the wheel. He announced, "This is good beer."

I reluctantly took the can, not wanting to take a sip. I was only a freshman in high school. I looked at Randy and started laughing, "I can't. Here, drink it for me."

Randy held out his hand. "You gotta try it. This is all we drink in Texas."

I was becoming frightened by the situation. I knew that the only way I would get back to the school dance was to do as Randy said. I took the beer from him and took a sip. A tiny bit of beer dribbled down my chin and onto my new dress. "Yuk," I said. "That tastes awful!" I opened the passenger door and spit out the beer. Feeling a bit lightheaded, I added, "Isn't it dangerous to drink and drive?"

From that moment on, I was more conscious of teenage drinking, but not as careful as I should have been. I was not surprised when Bill and his friends stopped at a liquor store after dinner, before heading to the prom. They purchased some cheap Andre champagne, even though they also were underage. Purchasing alcohol in the early '80s was simple. Most liquor stores didn't even card teens. I became a victim of peer pressure for a second time: I didn't want Bill's friends to disapprove of me. I became slightly intoxicated after the first couple sips, liking the taste of champagne more than beer. By the time we arrived at the prom, I was acting silly and slurring my words. My beautiful baby blue prom dress was disheveled. Bill escorted me to the picture-taking area. Hanging onto him, I could barely stand. I felt his anger mounting. I had embarrassed him by displaying a side of my personality that I hadn't even known existed. I had gotten angry, said horrible things to him in front of his friends. I lost control, and our relationship was tarnished.

Months later, shortly before Bill's graduation, I lay on my bed comparing the Sadie Hawkin's dance picture to the prom picture we had taken. I thought to myself, "No wonder Bill is disappointed in me; the prom was a disaster." I had done the exact thing that Bill loathed. I got drunk. I probably reminded him of his mother, embarrassing him in front of his friends. How would he ever forgive me? I was amazed by how quickly I changed. Once an innocent girl who liked to secretly waltz around the living room, I was now becoming a defiant teenager. One picture showed a happy girl, a shy girl who was afraid to stand too close to Bill. The next featured a girl who had made poor choices. I would keep the pictures as souvenirs of our time together, pictures documenting inexorable changes in my demeanor, personality, and manners—changes that were affecting my relationship with Bill.

CHAPTER EIGHT
PROMISE RING

Bill needed a job once he graduated from high school. His mother lost her job because she didn't show up for a night shift. They needed money to pay the rent. Bill was steadfast in looking for employment. He applied all over town, but only one place hired him. Bill got a job at Marie Callender's. He was going to bus tables before eventually moving up to server. Bill was excited about his new position. He seemed to relish the fact that he could help his mother pay the rent. Margaret got a new job as a nurse in another alcohol rehabilitation center. In the meantime, they were late on their rent and had to find another place to live. Bill seemed to forgive my questionable behavior at the prom. He came up to my house one day, a small, gray velvet box in his hands.

Bill at the Grand Canyon National Park.

I was in my parent's bathroom when I heard a knock on the bathroom door. I said, "Hi, I thought you were my brother. I was ready to yell at him for bothering me. I'm glad to see you instead. What are you holding?" I was excited to see proof of his love for me, noticing he was carrying a small ring box.

Bill held out his hand and said, "I bought this with my first paycheck. When I saw it, I thought of you. It's a promise ring."

I opened the small box and started crying. Inside was the most beautiful golden heart, with a small diamond inserted near the top of the ring. The ring looked like it cost a pretty penny. I was wondering how Bill could afford such an extravagant gift.

I hugged Bill and said, "I was worried you didn't love me after I acted so horribly at your prom. I embarrassed you. You bought me a ring?"

Bill lifted my chin and looked into my eyes, "I love you!"

I couldn't protest. I was hungry for his love to be returned. All this time I'd wondered if he felt the same love for me. I knew our relationship was not ideal, but Bill had given me a golden heart with a diamond to prove his love for me. I felt the same way, and wished that he had proposed marriage to me. "If only I were a couple of years older," I thought to myself. I giggled with delight and said, "Thank you. I will always wear this."

Bill kissed me gently on my lips. I wanted the moment to last forever. He said, "I have the afternoon off. Wanna go for a ride to Santa Barbara? My friend Al let me borrow his Jeep. I want to try out some trails I've heard about."

I agreed to go with him. I wanted to honor Bill's motive for giving me such an ideal gift. I'd never felt such immense love for another human being as I had at that moment, knowing the hurdles he would face due to spending money on a gift for me rather than helping his mother pay the rent.

The day was spent driving along the coast to Santa Barbara. What started out as an ideal day turned into a nightmare. I was fine until Bill insisted on taking the Jeep on the back roads of the Santa Barbara Mountains. Bill was excited to test fate once again. Again, I was too conservative for such a road trip. Bill drove the jeep down a dirt road located on the steep side of the mountain. He said to me while he was driving, "This is going to be fun. Wait here. I'm going to let the jeep idle while I put it in four-wheel drive."

I looked out the window and saw nothing but the vertical cliff dropping off about three hundred feet. I had my first anxiety attack in months, and said, "We can't four-wheel here. We'll fall down the mountain. This road's too narrow. Take me home, Bill. I'm scared." I felt as if I had changed into a little girl. I had been so mature that morning, accepting a ring from the boy I loved. Now, I was horrified that Bill was going to hotrod down the steep mountainside. He wasn't listening to me. He was hungry for indulgence. Bill's very nature dictated that he test fate, take leaps to defy physics. All I could think about was ending up injured. I was a novice when it came to four-wheel driving. My instinct dictated my behavior that day. Bill was invigorated by taking life to the extremes, and I was intolerant of his need to tempt fate, once again.

When he got back into the Jeep, I said, "Bill, I'll get out of this Jeep if you don't take me home. I don't care if I have to walk back. If we go much further we could tip over the edge of the mountain. I'm too young to die. We're going to be injured if we don't get out of here. Please Bill. I'm begging you!"

Bill and I had our first real argument that day. I was in hysterics by the time he got back to the highway. I was crying, threatening him, disputing why he would put someone that he supposedly loved in harm's way. I screamed, "You're insane for wanting to four-wheel drive on this mountain. I'll never forgive you for putting me in such danger!"

Bill's jaw tightened. I could see his jaw moving back and forth. I had mocked his ability to drive. By screaming, I had shown an incompatible side of my personality. I knew our relationship would never be the same.

Bill looked over at me and said, "My aunt is out of town at a conference. I have a key to her house. Do you want to stop and help me water her plants?"

I looked at him, mystified. "I guess so. I just want to get off this mountain."

Bill grinned at me smugly, "I guess I won't be taking you four-wheeling anytime soon. You're such a sissy!"

I nodded, agreeing, "I'll stick to safer sports like swimming."

Bill snickered, "I guess you'll want to go up to Lake Nacimiento, then. Al invited me to go water skiing with him and a couple friends."

I questioned him, a note of jealousy cracking my voice, "When?"

Bill chuckled, "I knew you'd want to go. The only thing is ... it might get a little dangerous out on the water."

I sighed, "At least I'm a good swimmer. I don't do good hanging over the side of steep cliffs. I've never mountain-climbed with a broken neck."

Bill said, "That would never happen. Besides, if it did, you know I'd carry you back up."

I glanced at him, "You can carry me into your aunt's house. Let's go. I think I peed my pants!"

Bill dropped me off at my house after spending a couple hours watering his aunt's plants. I felt bad that I ruined Bill's four-wheeling experience. The life that he wanted to live was too dangerous and intense for me. I kissed him and said,

"Thanks again for the ring. I'm sorry I got hysterical on the mountain. I felt the same way on the back of your motorcycle. I hope you aren't angry with me. I love the ring, and I love you."

Bill went back to his apartment that night. He was never unkind to me, even though I knew I infuriated him that day. I'd been inconsiderate of his feelings, but I was safe back at home and alive. All that mattered was the fact that I was still alive and the fact that I was wearing a golden heart on my finger, even if our personalities were different. I now had the greatest keepsake I could ask for, an token of Bill's love, a promise ring that I'd wear forever.

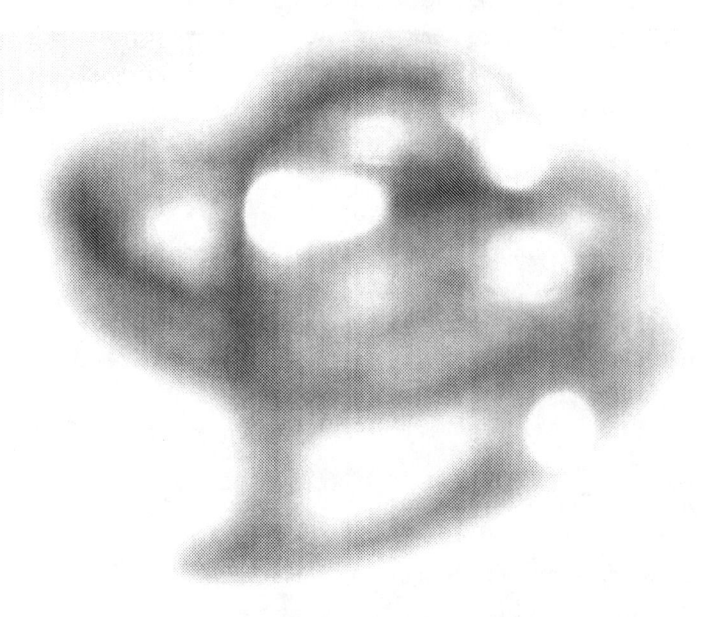

The actual promise ring that Bill gave me.

CHAPTER NINE
TEMPTING STRAWBERRY PIE

I turned sixteen in June, 1980. My life had taken an odd turn. My mother and father's marriage was ending after eighteen years, all because my father had walked in the front door one day and told my mother, "Patricia, I met the most beautiful blond today."

My mother, who was cooking in the kitchen, said, "Ryan, you better be careful. Women out there find you mighty attractive."

When I was alone in my room, I thought back to the time my family took the family to Simi Valley for my mother's dear friend's twenty-fifth wedding anniversary. I took my mother's friend's nephew out for a spin in our family's new green Volvo. We drove for hours around the town where I spent the first nine years of my life. By the time my father had made it halfway up Nob Hill, on our way home, the Volvo ran out of gas. We walked up the street to our house as a family, my father furious with my inability to take responsibility. When we got home, my father said, "I'm going to take the Porsche out and get some gas for the Volvo."

He left, never to return. My mother drove the moped with our housekeeper to look for my father, wanting to get her leased car back. She had her beauty shop clients to attend to the next day and had to be at work early the next morning. She needed her car.

Mom found her car parked in a cul-de-sac at the same condo development where my parents had invested. I often heard my mother say, "Those condos will pay for our children's education someday." My mom came face to face with my father's mistress as she was getting behind the wheel of her car. She never received such an indecent tongue-lashing from another human being as she had from my father's new love. My mother was heartbroken about her marriage ending, the family being ripped apart by an adulterous affair. The most difficult part of both of my parents' infidelity was the fact that we attended church regularly. My father was a Sunday school teacher. I felt that God was certainly putting us to the test.

My life changed when my dad left the family. My mother worked hard to save the only home we knew, the same one that the IRS almost seized due to non-payment of back taxes. We ate beans because my mother couldn't afford groceries. My mother told me one night, "Your father has left me deeply in dept. I can't afford to send you to private school anymore. I'll have to enroll you in Buena. At least you can be on the swim team, now."

I looked at my mother, large tears filling my eyes, and begged. "I'm not going to Buena. I want to graduate with my friends. I'll get a job at the Broadway. I'll make enough money to pay the tuition. I don't want to go to another school. Mother, don't make me change schools. I only have two years left. You make enough money at your shop. Why can't I stay with my friends?"

My mother replied sternly, "I sold the beauty shop months ago to pay for the property in Florence. I never said anything because I didn't want you to worry."

It was bad enough having my credit cards taken away, my father leaving the house, and my mother now dating a wealthy businessman. My life had taken a turn for the worse. The only thing holding me together was Bill's happy-go-lucky attitude about life. Now I was feeling insecure about losing him, too.

I spent my sixteenth birthday alone, a large birthday cake sitting on the table before me. I didn't get the car I had dreamed about all my life. I had proven to my parents that I was a good driver, but because their lives had gone in separate directions, I wasn't able to get my license. I sat at the Thomasville table my mother purchased many years before, the rich wood reminding me that life had once been fruitful.

Bill had to work the night of my sixteenth birthday, even though he promised to take me out. I was suspicious of him. My own insecurities and feelings of abandonment were making me angry and inconsiderate, not only of Bill, but of my friends, too. It must've been challenging to be around me. I angrily asked Bill one night on the phone, "Don't bother taking me out the night after my birthday. What good will it do if you can't be here to help me celebrate on the actual day?"

I was hurt, and I was taking my emotions out on Bill. Bill didn't deserve for me to inflict anger on him. He was an innocent bystander, who had his own family problems to deal with. He kept insisting that he take me out for dinner, saying, "I want to see you. I feel bad that I can't make it for your birthday. Can't I come over tomorrow night?"

I replied, resenting my new life, knowing I had responsibilities of my own, "I have to work tomorrow night so I can pay my high school tuition." Bill agreed to pick me up from work that next evening.

Bill didn't show up when my shift was over. He stood me up. This made me even sadder than spending my birthday alone. I started to worry that I was subconsciously pushing people away. I walked back into the employee entrance of the department store. Making a call at the pay phone, I dialed my mother's private line. I paid to have my own phone. My mother answered on the first ring, as if expecting me to call, "Hello?"

I spoke into the phone, out of breath from the stress of the situation and said, "Mom. Bill didn't pick me up. Can you come and get me?"

My mother said, "Honey, Bill lost his job tonight. He came up here and told me the whole story. He was so distraught over his being fired that he must have forgotten you were at work. He's on his way to get you. He should be there in a couple minutes."

Wanting my mother to explain more, I said, "Mom, what'd you say about Bill getting fired? Why did he lose his job? He was such a great employee. He loved that job!"

My mother said, "I think it's best that he tell you what happened. He'll be there soon. I promise you he'll be there soon."

I was in tears by the time my mother hung up the phone. Bill got fired from his job, and all I could focus on was the fact that he was late picking me up. I went back outside, glad that the summer months were finally here, although the fog was rolling in. The parking lot held few cars, as most of the shoppers and employees had gone home already. The sky was looking creepier. I could not escape my chilly feelings of doom. I wondered what had happened to Bill. I wished that my mother had divulged more information to me on the phone. I remembered Bill's enthusiasm when he had gotten his position at the restaurant. He relished in the fact that he was no longer dependant on his mother's income. He felt like a burden for most of his childhood, and now he could help her with the rent: "All the stress placed on my mother while I was in high school may have caused her to get off the wagon. Maybe, now that I'm working, she can relax a bit." Bill enjoyed going to work, interacting with other people. I thought about how my mother loved to be dramatic. Maybe she was exaggerating about Bill coming up to the house, crying on her shoulder. My mother was at a turning point in her own life. She liked other people's life dramas because they distracted her from her own life-a life of working hard and playing little.

After what seemed like an hour, Bill pulled his car up to the curb of the department store where I worked. I felt I had two choices: I could get angry with him for being late to pick me up, or I could be nice and silent, and give him a big fat kiss on the cheek. This would be a reassuring gesture that might boost his confidence. Through the fog, which had frightened me earlier, I saw a familiar white car pull up to the curb. I felt relieved to see him. He smiled as he stopped the car, bending over to open the passenger door for me. I suffered the familiar weakness in my knees, the same weakness I'd felt every day since I'd met Bill. He had some type of power over me. He made my heart swell, leaving me at a loss of words. Every trauma I experienced this past year—my parents divorce, having to work to pay for tuition, giving up the former luxuries I'd known—had all been worth it. I still had Bill.

I pulled the swinging door open so I could sit down on the blue vinyl seat. I glanced over at him shyly and said, "I was worried about you. I called my mother to come get me. Mom said that something happened to you tonight. Do you want to talk about it?" Knowing that Bill needed a reassuring glance, I bent over and kissed his cheek. Wanting him to trust me with his innermost secrets, but knowing that I was emotionally inept at dealing with many events that took place in our lives, like the alcoholism and the divorce, I still wanted him to confide in me. I was dying to know what happened, and hoping that he wouldn't hesitate to tell me. I could tell he was hurt, but happy that my mother had given me some type of warning. Being callous at times, expecting much more from people than they were willing to give, I would have to drum up some patience. Thank goodness my mother told me why Bill hadn't been on time to pick me up. Knowing about Bill's job, I could avoid a fight that might have ended our relationship.

Closing the door, I tried to speak as gently as I could. Bill was proud of his first car. He boasted about the great paint job and other such details. He could've been driving a cart with oxen, and I wouldn't have cared. He pulled away from the curb at a high speed, leaving a skid mark in his path. I could tell he didn't want to talk, and I was hoping I wouldn't experience another anxiety attack. He was in his own world, a world into which I would have to gain access. I turned to him as he stopped at a light near the mall's entrance. "My mother told me that you came up to my house tonight. She said you were upset. I don't want to beat around the bush. I want to know what happened. Did you lose your job tonight?"

Bill, a rebel in disguise?

I could see tears streaming down his face. Bill was too proud. He had to deal with too many emotions from the life events that had taken him to this moment. He drove swiftly through the streets of Ventura, a dramatic silence filling his car. I said, "Bill, the silence is frightening me. Please explain what happened at your job. I don't want to hear about your job from my mother. I want to know. I need to know. I can help you. I want you to know that I'm here for you. Please don't put up a wall. I love you."

Bill was having a difficult time communicating with me. My overbearing nature seemed to be having the opposite effect on Bill's emotions. I was enthusiastically trying to play the role of Bill's mom. I knew that silence was the best strategy for the time being. If I pushed Bill to tell me what happened to his job, he would develop more resentment toward me. I held him back from many things that he enjoyed in life: four-wheeling, his time with his friends, and his eccentric nature. He was eccentric because he liked to test fate. I looked down at the golden heart with the small diamond. The diamond sparkled. The ring was on my finger for a reason. I had to keep calm. Bill gave me a promise ring. We would surely make it as a couple through this roadblock that Bill refused to talk about. Bill wouldn't say a word to me on the drive home. He drove his car with speed and precision through the foothills of Ventura. I was more hurt with each curve he drove around. I thought, "Doesn't Bill trust me with his feelings?"

I looked over at him, making a second attempt to find a way into his heart, "Bill, why're you so quiet tonight? I'd like to help you, if you would just open and tell me what happened."

Bill couldn't look at me. He focused on the curvy road as he admitted, "I lost my job."

I was shocked and could see that just those few words were difficult for him to get off his tongue. I looked over at him, memorizing his profile in my mind. Amazed at his features, I started to cry because I was happy that Bill was speaking to me, "What happened?" I was genuinely concerned.

Bill, still too embarrassed to look at me, said, "Another employee and I were in the prep area. He had an idea about tasting the strawberry pies. The next thing we knew, we had eaten two full pies. They were so good. The strawberries were so fresh. I couldn't help myself. I ate a whole pie. My manager walked in. He asked us what we were doing in the prep area. My mouth was full of strawberry pie. I couldn't answer him. I started laughing. The situation was serious, but all I could do was laugh. I got fired tonight. I was fired for eating a strawberry pie."

All I could think that night as I lay in bed was how great temptation was in people's lives. Temptation was everywhere. My parents were tempted by sex and money, I was tempted by Bill, and Bill was tempted by strawberry pie. What would life be like if people avoided temptation? If my family and I had, our lives would never had taken such drastic turns.

Bill gave me a birthday card that night using the nickname he had for me. It was a sweet gesture, even though he was in so much pain. The card read in his exact words, some of which I later asked him to interpret:

Dearest Spamilla, I do too. You should know what that means, considering the way you start your letters. I just got one in the mail today, and it was very, very, very sweet. It also made me want to write you back, and it really isn't as hard as I thought it would be, so maybe I'll write more often—as long as you keep up your part, which you do. I love you (oops). Sorry, just felt like saying that (and I mean it). I told you I'm not good at this. I lov #@—see, I almost did it again—but you know I do. I hope you don't show this to your friends or mine—well I guess you can show it to Cindy and Joe. Well, I'll talk to ya soon and I hope you still love me even after this stupid card. PS—If you go to Italy, don't forget to give me directions how to get there, because you know I'll be on my way—and you know why. I love you. Happy Birthday, Sweet 16. Love, Bill.*

CHAPTER TEN
OIL

Bill was devastated about losing his job. He and his mother needed the money more than I knew. Bill went back to the restaurant and defended himself to his manager. He asked for another chance, saying, "I know what I did was wrong. The pie looked so good. I knew that strawberries grow in abundance in Oxnard. I didn't think that my eating a strawberry pie would really impact sales of this restaurant. I just want you to know that I'm sorry. Can I have my job back so I can prove that I'm not a bad person?" Bill's manager was relentless. He wouldn't give Bill a second chance.

Bill spent his spare time looking for a new job. One day, while looking in the Sunday Star Free Press, Bill saw an ad that caught his eye. A major oil company was hiring workers for their offshore rigs. Bill had all the qualifications mentioned, and he knew the job was something he could do. Bill was excited about working offshore. He was also looking forward to the pay, which was far more than he made at the restaurant. Bill had renewed hopes for his future. Before long, Bill called me to tell me that he had gotten a job as a roughneck. He would be working on an oil rig off the coast near Carpinteria. "They hired me on the spot," he told me. "I'll be making a lot more money. I can't wait to start!"

I spoke into the phone, trying not to sound overly protective, "What do you mean working offshore? Isn't that dangerous?"

Bill started his new job a couple of weeks later. I never saw him so happy. The first thing he did when he got his first paycheck, besides help his mother pay the rent, was to trade in his large white car for a Jeep Renegade. Bill drove the Jeep up to my house, excited to show off his new vehicle. He knocked on my front door. When I answered, Bill said, "I have a surprise for you. Come with me. I want to show you something."

I couldn't believe that Bill gotten rid of the white car we'd had so many good times in without consulting me first and said, "Bill, what happened to your car?" Bill looked at me proudly and said, "I make more money than I know what to do with. I've always wanted a Jeep CJ-7. This is a sports model—look at the soft-top roof. It's so easy to take off! Joe and I already took it four-wheeling. It was fun. Do you want to take a drive in it?"

I looked at Bill, afraid that the money had already had an impact on his life. "Sure," I said, remembering the time he took me four-wheeling in Santa Barbara and thinking, "Oh no, not again!"

My mother was excited for Bill and his new job. When she saw his new Jeep, she said, "Wow. That's beautiful. I bet you have a lot of fun in this. Does it have four-wheel drive?" She went on to ask about his commute and about how he was liking the new job.

Bill answered each of my mother's questions with enthusiasm. His commute wasn't that long, and he worked four days on, three days off, so he didn't have to drive it every day. The work was dangerous, but he had been trained well. He and his fellow roughnecks drove up to the pier in Carpinteria to catch the ferry. If the waves were choppy, they took a helicopter. Getting to the rig was the tricky part, because the weather could be unpredictable. The oil rigs looked close from shore, but in reality they were about five miles out, in the deeper part of the ocean. "I could tell you some stories," he concluded, "but I don't think Pam would like any of them."

We went for a long drive that afternoon. Bill wanted to show me where he caught his ferry to work. I was amazed at the area, one that I was unfamiliar with. We turned off the main road leading into Carpinteria. We drove down a one-lane, tree-lined road that led to a large dirt parking lot. An amazing number of cars, trucks, and Jeeps were parked in the lot. All of them had some sort of saltwater corrosion. I asked Bill, when I saw the rusty cars, "Your Jeep won't rust like those cars, will it?"

Bill smiled at me and said, "If it does, I'll just buy a new one."

I knew from the comment that Bill changed. A sudden feeling of anxiety swept over me, and I wondered if Bill would trade me in for a new model, too. I felt like I lost control of my boyfriend and the way he was now treating me. He was now a grimy thief of crude ocean resources, helping the oil companies make more money so that people could drive more cars and heat larger homes, thus creating more air pollution. His new life as a roughneck would be dangerous, demanding, and desolate.

CHAPTER ELEVEN
THE ALARM CLOCK

I hugged Bill and gave him a passionate kiss, saying, "You're such a good skier." Bill, a natural athlete, excelled at all sports. He looked at me and said, "I've been skiing since I was a child. My mother used to take me to the slopes before I could walk. One time she took me to one of the resorts. She signed me up for ski lessons. By the end of the day I was skiing down diamond runs. I was only six." Bill made me laugh. We were in Big Bear, skiing for the weekend. My mother and her new boyfriend, Maurice, had taken us.

Maurice was a generous man. One day he had called my mother and said, "You and Pam get your stuff together. I'll be at your house in less than an hour."

My mother was confused, and said, "Why do you want us to get our things together? What're you planning?"

Maurice said, "I'm hungry for a hamburger. I know this great little restaurant in San Francisco. I'd like for us to fly up there today for one of those hamburgers."

My mother came into my room and said, "Maurice is flying us up to San Francisco for a hamburger. We'll be back tonight. Get your things together."

Maurice owned a cabin up in Big Bear, where we were staying for the weekend. I invited Bill even though he didn't care for Maurice. Bill was devastated when my family broke up. My mother met Maurice when she drove around Ventura on Christmas Eve, looking for a condo to move into. Maurice happened to be a land developer. He was at the new development site when my mother got there, and their courtship followed. My mother was impressed by Maurice's dedication to his work: he was both a land developer and a lawyer. Maurice had wrapped his arms around my mother that day, telling her that he would protect and care for her, helping her through her troubled times.

He wanted my mother to forget that my father had ever existed. She still loved my father, in a way, but Maurice had taken her away from a life of destitution, given her elaborate gifts, and taken her on enjoyable vacations. Maurice doted on my mother, gave her ego the boost it had so needed after my father left. My mother stayed loyal to Maurice even when my father came to the condo to reconcile with her. Maurice locked the door and said, "Don't answer the door. I've got a gun. I'll use it." My mother did exactly as she was told. She cared for my father and didn't want him to be hurt or killed even though he left her for another woman. When I heard that story years later I couldn't help but cry.

Bill and I were enjoying our time skiing the slopes and staying in Maurice's posh cabin until Bill said, "We've got to drive back to Ventura tonight. I've got to be at the pier at five tomorrow morning."

I looked at Bill. "You can't be serious. We aren't supposed to be back until Sunday night. This is the last part of winter break. I want to go skiing one more day. Can't you call in sick?"

Bill, who now looked stressed, said, "I've only been working on the rig for less than six months. I'm still on probation. I don't want to lose my job again. Let's ask your mother if we can drive her Porsche. She can get a ride back with Maurice."

I couldn't believe that I had to cut my ski vacation short, but I didn't want to argue with Bill, so I said only, "I wish you would've told me earlier." I would drive to the ends of the earth for him, so this wasn't that much of a conflict. If we went back early, we would have the whole house to ourselves. I was now motivated to leave early because I had ulterior motives. I looked at Bill and said, "Let's go back to the cabin and ask my mother. She knows how important your job is to you. I'm sure she'll let you drive her car back to Ventura." I didn't know, however, if she would let *me* drive. I had recently gone to a party and had too much to drink. I'd taken a corner too wide and ended up denting the front fender. I had also burned a hole in her leather seat—I wasn't supposed to smoke in her car, but I did. My mother would never let me drive her car again after that.

Bill at Big Bear

Bill drove the Porsche at top speed. We made it home in two hours. I was exhausted, yet happy to have the whole house to ourselves, the same house my mother kept after her divorce. She was able to keep the house we grew up in by purchasing my father's share of the equity. My father ended up with two condos near the development where he had fatefully knocked on the door that day, to be greeted by the "beautiful blonde" who changed all of our lives. My mother had come home one day to find the door barricaded by tape labeled "IRS Seizure." My parents had been audited yearly for the last five years of their marriage. My mother wondered if deceit would follow her forever. Every time she turned a corner, she found that her finances were unjustly dispersed. Her domicile was being threatened. She had thought that all she had to do was buy my father out. My father had said, "I'll give you the house, because I want the kids to grow up in the only home they know."

Once the taxes were resolved, the seizure tape was removed. My mother credited the seizure removal to a letter she wrote to the President, who also happened to be a California resident. "I wrote that my husband left me for another woman," she liked to tell people, "and I was left raising my two children. I was trying to keep them in the lifestyle that they had been accustomed, but found that the fruits of my labor only went so far. I came home one day and the tape was gone." My mother said that was the best day of her life. She had been able to keep the only home that we kids had ever known. Even though there were some pretty bad memories there about quarrels in which the police were called, there were some good memories, too like all of our birthday parties, dates picking us up for school events—and divine view of Ventura. "I hope that we'll enjoy this home for many years to come—even if we have to eat beans for the rest of our lives to pay the mortgage."

When we arrived back at Nob Hill, I walked into the dining room and looked out the sliding glass door at the bright city lights. The view was spectacular. I remembered that Bill had asked me to make sure the alarm clock was set for four in the morning. I made it a point to go back to my room and set the clock before falling asleep. I walked over to the liquor cabinet and looked inside. I was amazed that my mother had been able to keep such a vast array of liquor. I knew that Maurice was helping my mother, purchasing groceries and different California wine varietals. I was too tired to indulge that night. I walked back to my bedroom, lying down on the waterbed and hoping I wouldn't disturb Bill, who was sleeping peacefully. I lay down beside him, forgetting to set the alarm clock.

The sun woke Bill the next morning. He jumped out of bed and said, "What time is it?"

I looked up sleepily and said, "I don't know."

Waves sloshed across the waterbed as he leapt up to put on his clothes. "I'll probably lose my job! I can't believe you forgot to set the clock like I asked you to. You want me to lose my job, don't you? You've never supported me. You think it's dangerous, that I'll get hurt. You wanted me to be late so I'll get fired!"

I sat up and tried to defend myself, "No. I forgot to set the alarm clock last night. I didn't do it intentionally. I went out to the dining room to look at the view. I was thankful that we made it home safely. I was happy to be home. I was going to get something to drink. I decided to get some sleep instead. I totally forgot. I'm sorry."

There were tears in my eyes as Bill ran out of the house. All I could do was cry at the sound of him slamming the front door. I ran out to the same sliding glass door that I looked out the night before and stepped out onto the balcony, desperately yelling, "Bill. Come back. You can call your boss. Please don't leave. I love you and would never try to get you fired." I knew that the dull roar of the Jeep's engine would keep Bill from hearing my plea.

Bill had every right to be angry. His job was at stake, and he had yet to complete the probationary period that was required to secure his position and to receive a raise. But Bill wasn't the only one who accused me of wrongdoing. Maurice's maid told my mother that Bill and I had run through the house naked and raided the liquor cabinet. She said she'd seen us because she had come upstairs to see who was home. "I didn't expect you till the next day. I heard footsteps. It was dark. I was frightened that somebody was robbing the house."

This wasn't the first dispute that had happened in the house. It probably wouldn't be the last. Maurice even said, "When I see that boy again, I'm going to let him know what I think. He should be more responsible than that."

I looked over at my mother, wondering what she saw in this man, and said, "Bill spent the night because we got home late. We didn't run through the house naked, and we didn't drink your liquor. Bill fell asleep in my room, and I forgot to set the alarm clock. Now Bill is going to lose his job. I would hope that you don't mention to Bill what Maria said. It would only upset him more. I'll take full responsibility for what happened." I never felt such fear and dismay. I was going to be grounded, and Bill was going to lose his job. My future looked as bleak and dismal as the fog rolling in off the ocean.

CHAPTER TWELVE
THIEF OF HEARTS

I didn't hear from Bill for two weeks after the alarm clock incident. I blamed my mother's boyfriend. I told my mother, "I bet Bill called, and Maurice gave him a tongue lashing about what Maria said. Can't you ask Maurice if he yelled at Bill? I really need to know if Bill is staying away because Maurice told him to!"

My mother looked at me, still upset about Maria's story. I disliked Maria for telling on us and made it a point to say "green card" when I saw her upstairs cooking or ironing. Maria would look at me and say, "No, Pam, no." I was going through emotional changes and didn't seem to have control. I wasn't prepared to break up with my boyfriend. I knew that I would be devastated. Even though I called Bill daily, he never returned my calls. I left nearly the same message on his answering machine every day: "Bill, this is Pam. Please call me. I want to know what happened with your job. Were you able to make it to the ferry that day? I'm worried about you."

I tried to rationalize his not giving me the attention that I craved. I knew that Bill didn't care for Maurice and that he disproved of my parents divorce. He had a difficult time understanding his own mother and why she would choose to date men that she worked with. Both of our lives were dysfunctional, he said. "Your mother, my mother, they deserve better, you know? Why do they go for men like Maurice and Rudy? Those men are pond scum." Bill tried to tell his mother how he felt, but she wouldn't listen. He even had a talk with my mom about Maurice. "Why would she be attracted to an overweight man like Maurice who threatened your father when he came to Maurice's home trying to patch things up?" he would ask indignantly. According to Bill, my mother freely admitted that Maurice's money was part of the reason she liked him. She also said that she felt safe in his arms, and that she enjoyed taking trips with him, eating in fancy restaurants, and sailing in his sailboat. Margaret's attraction to Rudy confused Bill still more. "He doesn't even have any money. But my mother told me that she enjoyed having men be dependent on her…. My mother and your mother are alike in some ways. They've both picked seriously peculiar men. The only couple I know that's lasted through the years are my grandparents."

I replied to Bill, "It's gotta be the money."

I missed Bill. I hoped that he wasn't injured. I told my mother, "Do you think Bill got hurt on the oil rig? He could be in the hospital."

My mother replied, "Pamela, don't be silly. If that happened, you'd be the first to know." I picked up my mother's phone and was beginning to call again, when I stopped. "I have this funny feeling in my gut. Something isn't right. This isn't like Bill not to call me."

My mother looked up at me and said, "Pamela, put the phone down. Trust me. Your instinct is correct. You come by it naturally. I had the same feelings when your father had the affair. I knew something wasn't right. I remember sitting on our bed one night, asking him if he was having an affair. That was probably the stupidest question that I could have ever asked. Look where that question has led our family." My mother paused, remembering. "We've been ripped apart at the seams. Your father had tears in his eyes. I'd never seen him cry. He looked straight into my eyes and confirmed my suspicions. I'd already known before he answered me. My gut told me that something wasn't right."

She had asked my father if he was in love with the woman he'd met while knocking on doors, and he'd said yes. "My heart stopped," my mother continued. "I'd never been more devastated. I lost thirty pounds. I'll always remember going into the courthouse for our divorce. I got into the elevator to go up to see the judge. The elevator smelled of perfume. I thought to myself, I hope that John didn't bring that woman. I got off of the elevator and there they were, seated hand in hand. She had the reddest lips I'd ever seen. I'll never forget that moment. Once we got in to see the judge, I got down on my hands and knees and begged your father to stop the divorce proceedings."

I placed the telephone back in the cradle and said, "Mother, please don't talk like that. The whole thing is horrible. It'll only make you sad. Dad was probably going through a midlife crisis." My mother's story was also making me sad—sad and anxious. I had seen very little of my father since the divorce. I still couldn't believe that he was with a woman who felt so threatened by his children. She didn't want him to have anything to do with us, and he seemed to accept her terms. We couldn't go over there, and he didn't take us on the weekends. Maybe he never loved us. Maybe Bill never loved me. "Men," I said out loud, "You can't live with them. You can't live without them."

My mother agreed with me—"Isn't that the truth!" I looked down at my golden promise ring. I knew that Bill had, at least, loved me at one time—otherwise, I wouldn't have the ring. Maybe Bill was going through a change similar to my father's, a mid-life crisis of sorts.

I walked back to my bedroom. I wanted to know what Bill was doing with his life. I wondered why he didn't want me in his life anymore, but decided that I wouldn't let him get away so easily. I thought back to when we met and wondered if Bill and his mother had had to find another place to live because the lady had seen us in the bedroom. He never told me if she saw us, but then again, he never told me a lot of things. I began to get dressed. I decided that I would drive my mother's car to Bill's apartment. I needed to confront him. I had given Bill the benefit of the doubt many times before in our relationship. This time I felt more insecure than ever. I needed to talk to Bill.

I closed my bedroom door and asked my mother if I could use her car for a couple of hours.

My mother looked up from her typewriter. She had sold the beauty shop and started a home-based business typing divorce papers for her clients. She said, "Okay."

I knew when I started backing the sleek brown Porsche out of the garage, which I was entering uncharted waters, confronting the boy I loved. I knew it was wrong to go chasing after a boy, but if I was going to function in life, I needed to know why Bill was ignoring me. I glanced in the rearview mirror. I looked good. I looked charming. I looked polished. Bill would have a difficult time rejecting me and saying farewell.

I drove the Porsche 924 fast, my heart pounding, my knees shaking. I anticipated the reunion I'd have with Bill. I drove down Victoria Avenue with precision, hoping that I wouldn't get a speeding ticket. I passed the courthouse where my parent's had finalized their divorce. I felt faint as I drove into the parking lot of Bill's apartment complex. I parked and unfastened my seat belt, then thought better of parking so far away from his apartment. I wanted to park closer, just in case I needed to leave in a rush.

As I was pulling forward to park in his apartment's designated covered space, I saw two people walking toward Bill's apartment. I inched closer and recognized Bill, walking to his apartment with a tall, thin girl with curly brown hair. I was glad that I had made the decision to stay in my mother's car. Bill was with another girl. I hesitated, not wanting to park the car. I wanted to drive off, but I had to speak with Bill. I had to ask him why he hadn't been calling me. I rolled down the window and yelled his name, "Bill!" He had already seen my car. He whispered something into the girl's ear and came toward the car. I noticed that the girl went ahead of him into his apartment, opening the door as if she had been there many times before. Bill came over to the window and said, "What's up?"

I looked at him and said, "Who is she?"

Bill looked at me and said, "She's a friend."

I didn't need an explanation. I put the car in reverse and sped off. This time I didn't care if I got a ticket. When I got home, my mother looked at my tear-stained face and asked, "What happened?"

"I drove down to see Bill. I saw him with another girl. They were walking into his apartment. Here, you take this ring. I don't want to wear it anymore." I ran to my room and slammed the door. All I wanted was to feel safe in a familiar setting, my bedroom. I knew that my luck had taken a fatal turn. I would never survive the failure of this relationship.

I caught Bill red-handed with another girl. I was glad that I hadn't made a scene when I saw them. I remembered my mother telling me that my father's girlfriend had accused her of not possessing any class. I knew that having class was extremely important. I was proud of myself for handling the situation with dignity and class. I had driven off without explanation. I hadn't gotten angry. Bill couldn't see me crying in my bedroom. I remembered the shocked look on Bill's face as he walked toward the Porsche. He looked handsome, and I knew no other girl could resist him. He was wearing his Levis 501s, which made his legs look long and slim. He was tan from working out in the ocean. When he bent down to talk to me, all I could think about was how he had bruised my ego and how I felt like a fool. As I drove home, I thought I would somehow have to pull myself together and survive. I was a senior in high school, and my grades were suffering. If I wanted to graduate, I would have to concentrate on school. I wished this emotional time with Bill had happened after I'd finished high school. I had a job that I needed to concentrate on in order to pay my tuition. I would have to muster a strength to overcome this wretched time that I wasn't sure existed.

CHAPTER THIRTEEN
A SLAP IN THE FACE

Bill called me a couple of weeks later. He told me on the phone, "I feel real bad about what happened. Maybe we can go for a drive so I can talk with you."

I thought about all of the new emotions I'd been experiencing during the past couple of weeks. I fantasized about Bill and the curly-haired girl making love in his apartment. I was jealous. I was possessive of Bill because I was still, after all, his girlfriend. A part of me didn't want him because he hurt me. I didn't want to be hurt again, but I would meet him. I replied, "Tomorrow night I get off work at eight. I'll be home by eight thirty."

Bill spoke into the phone, "I'll be there."

I didn't want Bill to pick me up at work. He had disappointed me a couple times by not showing up. I couldn't rely on him not to leave me stranded in the dark parking lot. But when I hung up the phone, I was smiling. I hadn't felt that happy in a month. Bill wanted to talk to me. I wondered if the conversation would be friendly or emotional. I knew I would be vulnerable, but I would try not to be grouchy and nag Bill about sabotaging our relationship.

He came over to pick me up the next evening. I'd been anticipating the meeting and had even purchased a new outfit. The employee discount was nice, but I missed the days when I used my parents' charge card at the store. I now paid cash for all my transactions, being a bit too young for a checking account. My favorite hobby, besides obsessing over Bill, was shopping. I loved to shop. I missed shopping the way that I used to when my parents were together. I now lived on a tight budget. I only made enough money to cover my school tuition, my personal phone, and gas for the yellow VW Bug I finally purchased. I looked in the mirror. My new outfit flattered my tall frame. Thoughts of what my mother would say filled my head: "I made all my outfits when I was growing up. I went to fashion designing school. I'm gifted in the domestic department. All my creations were handmade..." I started laughing. I *wasn't* gifted in the domestic department, and my mother was too busy to teach me those arts.

I heard the doorbell ring. I was hopeful that the evening would go smoothly. I would make it a point not to henpeck Bill about the girl I'd seen him with. He most likely wanted to apologize and get back together with me, but I wouldn't be easily swayed. He probably couldn't live without me; possibly he wanted to marry me. I would have to make it a long engagement, because I still needed to finish high school. Such fantasies I had-so far from the truth.

I closed my bedroom door as I walked out to the entryway. I walked lightly on the marble tile, as I didn't want to trip on its slick surface. Bill looked more handsome than ever. He was dressed in jeans and a blue chambray long-sleeved shirt. A feeling of indecision swept over me. I didn't know if I should kiss him or shake his hand. I knew what I wanted to do, but I also knew that our relationship had taken a hiatus. Bill had been heartless toward me. He dated someone behind my back, and if it hadn't been for me driving up and seeing him with another girl, I would have never known.

I looked into Bill's sparkling, still mischievous eyes and said, "You made it!"

Bill looked down at me knowingly, "Of course I made it."

I was filled with nervousness as I said, "I thought maybe you had better things to do." I laughed at the many possible interpretations of my comment, wanting to keep the conversation light. The last thing that I wanted to have happened was shouting scenario that had been played out so many times.

Bill reached out for my hand, saying, "I hope you don't mind the top off the Jeep. It's a nice evening, not too cold. Let's take a drive." Bill wrapped his arm around me as he walked me down the sidewalk and stairs toward his Jeep. He opened the door for me and said, "Watch your step. I'll turn the heater on. I've got a jacket in the backseat."

I tried to act nonchalant, but was perplexed and said, "That's okay. I'm fine." I didn't want to wear Bill's clothing. Having his garments wrapped around me would bring back too many memories. I had to be strong. I had to negotiate without giving away that I knew he was using me.

Bill started the engine and asked, "Where would you like to go? I need to get back soon, because I have to work tomorrow. We could stay close to your house where the view's so nice. I know this neat place where they're building homes. It's secluded and close by. We could go there if you want."

I looked over at Bill and smiled, saying, "How do you know this area so well?"

Bill shifted gears, trying not to drive too fast, and said, "I've got a friend who's in construction. He's building homes on the next hill over in Clearpoint. We can park under the stars and talk."

I knew Clearpoint well because I used to walk by the area before Cynthia's mom had started giving me rides. I decided to reach for Bill's jacket in the backseat. The wind was chilly once we started driving. As I put his jacket around me, I said, "Clearpoint's fine. I've always wanted to drive up to the houses. I've heard they're nice."

Bill parked in a still-vacant lot. He stopped the engine and said, "I've missed you."

I looked away from him, not wanting to cry, and said, "I missed you, too. I've been confused lately. After I saw you with that girl, I didn't know what to think. Why didn't you break up with me if you wanted to date other girls?"

Bill opened his door and said, "Come out here. Let's sit on the hood of the Jeep. It'll keep you warm."

It was dark and spooky, and I wondered out loud, "Isn't our being here illegal? Couldn't a patrol car come by?"

Bill pulled me close and kissed me tenderly, saying, "You worry too much."

I tried not to let the kiss make an imprint on my heart. Bill was being his usual impetuous, gregarious, and loving self, and I was incapable of making a decision. What Bill was about to do to me was not only improper, it was impulsive. But my soft heart proved immune to reason. I looked at Bill and said, "I love you."

Bill dropped me off a couple of hours later. I was mesmerized. Being with Bill affected my thoughts. I forgot to ask Bill if he was still my boyfriend. We didn't do much talking—our time had been spent exploring the stars. I got inside my house, my heart torn. My mother said, "Can I borrow your brush?"

I said, "Sure. It's in my purse." Shortly after looking for my purse and not being able to find it, I realized that I'd left my purse in Bill's Jeep. I had been too immersed in intimate intoxication to think about gathering my belongings. I headed back out to the car.

My mother looked up as I was leaving. "Use your instinct this time. Don't let your heart interfere."

I said, "Mom! Stick with divorces. Don't ever become an evangelist."

I rushed down to Bill's apartment and knocked on his door. After a couple of long minutes waiting outside in the cold, Bill answered the door, a curious look on his face. "Hi. What's up?"

I was wondering why Bill wouldn't open the door and let me in. Then it dawned on me, and I said suspiciously, "Why won't you invite me in? Is there another girl with you?"

Bill stepped outside and closed his apartment door behind him, saying, "I'm just tired. I have to work tomorrow."

I looked into the eyes that minutes before had deceived me and said, "I came down here to get my purse. I left it in your jeep."

Bill stepped back into his apartment and closed the door. I stood there dumbfounded on his porch. A couple of minutes later, he stepped back outside with my purse and said, "I was going to drop this off tomorrow before my shift."

I took the purse from him and put the strap over my shoulder. With my free hand, I slapped his face as hard as I could. I drove home thinking that Bill was the biggest creep I'd ever met. I later learned that my instincts were correct. Bill had a girl in his apartment, and not just any girl. This was a girl who I'd gone to elementary school with, a girl I used to call a friend. A girl Bill met at a party.

CHAPTER FOURTEEN
PAMELA '82, EUROPE FOR YOU!

I lay on my bed, thinking about the lack of guidance I had in my life. I was devastated over my relationship with Bill. My mother knocked on my bedroom door. "Can I come in?"

I looked up at her and whispered, "Sure."

My mother sat on the edge of the bed and said, "I'm worried about you. You don't seem like yourself lately. I haven't seen you smile in weeks. I know that finding Bill with someone else was difficult. It's the most difficult experience that you may ever face. But look what happened to me. Somehow I've picked myself up and tried to move on. You either move on or you become depressed, possibly suicidal. I don't want you to think like that. You've got your whole life ahead of you."

I sat up a bit, wanting my mother to leave me alone, and said, "I don't know how you did it, Mom. You seem to have forgotten Dad. You met Maurice. He takes you on European holidays. He takes you sailing on the weekends. Do you ever sit back and reflect?"

My mother looked at me critically, saying, "Of course I reflected. What good did it do me? I lost so much weight that the wind could have blown me over. What more could I have done? I would've died if I'd reflected much more.... Your father wanted the house, the cars, and supposedly the kids. I rose above it all with the strength of God. I don't see your father putting any effort into raising you two. He should be here now giving you some parental guidance. He doesn't realize how Bill's actions have distressed you. Your father has dismissed his duties as a parent.... In a sense, I've been an only parent since you were born. The divorce was probably due long before it happened. I always felt that your father was incapable of loving us."

I looked at my mother. Part of me resented her for causing the breakup of my family. I recently learned that she had played her own role in the breakup, conducting an affair with my father's best friend because she "wanted more out of life." I said, "I think the big part of breaking up with someone is the fact that people don't give themselves due time to confront their emotions. I feel like I was one of Bill's conquests. He never communicated with me. He never broke up with me. He just started dating other people." I thought this was probably an effort to compensate for his own emotions. He seemed so uncomfortable with commitment; he changed since he started working on the oil rigs. "I heard he's dating a girl whose father works for the sheriff's department. That means he's dated four girls in the past six months."

My mother came over to give me a hug. I shrugged. I didn't want any expression of love. My mother tried to be critical, covering up her own feelings of rejection by saying, "We all want that gallant knight in shining armor to sweep us off of our feet. This is a learning experience for you. You can either hold a grudge about your father and Bill, or you can ditch the heartache." My mother paused to catch her breath before continuing her impassioned lecture. My emotions were a hindrance, holding me back from managing my life. I should not listen to hearsay and gossip; they would only hurt me. I should stop blaming Bill. He was behaving like a boy his age should behave. He was too young to get married and was sowing his oats. I should be thankful for the time we'd had together. He was exploring his options. It has nothing to do with me. "He'll be back," my mother predicted. "Look at the pattern of your relationship with him. He's never succeeded at being away from you for a long time. You should be patient with him." Maybe he changed since he started working on the oil rigs, but every job changes people in some way. "Look at me. I used to be a beautician who owned my own business. Now I type divorces for people. Every phone call I take changes me. My heart breaks when I hear the stories, some being much worse than my own. I've changed a bit, too. Bill has an extremely dangerous job. Maybe he realizes that and wants to live life to the fullest."

I looked at my mother in amazement. I didn't want to hear that I needed to be patient and supportive of Bill. I needed a strategy for survival. I asked my mother one last question before she went back to her typewriter, "What about the promise ring? What should I do with it?" I looked down at the ring that I had retrieved from my mother's jewelry box. It was still on my finger, placed there moments before Bill came to pick me up the night I slapped his face. Little did I know that my mother was secretly creating a pillow for me that said, "Pam, '82 Europe for you."

My high-school graduation gift, 1982

CHAPTER FIFTEEN
MY GRADUATION DAY, CLASS OF 1982

I was finally graduating from high school. I made it. I was excited to be graduating with my best friends. The morning of my graduation ceremony, I woke up with a sense of tranquility. I went out to the kitchen to eat a bit of breakfast. My mother was already up. She cooked me a special breakfast of pecan waffles and scrambled eggs. My mother loved to cook. I remembered the brunches that we'd shared as a family on Sundays, Mom cooking or taking us to restaurants in the area. We often drove up the coast to the Biltmore in Santa Barbara for brunch. My mother read my mind, saying, "We're not going to the Biltmore, but I have a surprise I think you'll enjoy." My mother had a twinkle in her eye.

I had no idea why, and said, "I'll drive by myself. We're taking a class photo in front of the church. After that, we'll have a graduation mass. Make sure that you get to the church early so you can get a good seat. Is Dad coming?"

My mother looked up from pouring me a glass of orange juice and said, "I haven't talked to him. I'm proud of you. I don't want anything to spoil your day. I'm sure that your father means well. If he doesn't show up, don't take it personally. He loves you. You must always remember that." Then, smiling, she told me about my surprise. "I'm going to meet Cynthia. She wants to see you graduate!" Cynthia moved during our sophomore year, and we had lost touch. "I'm sure she wishes she could be graduating beside you."

I hugged my mom and said, "Yay! I can't wait to see her!"

I kept telling myself to not take anything that happened that day personally. I would pretend to be happy even if Bill or my father didn't participate in the days' festivities. After all, how could I expect Bill to attend when we were no longer a couple? I was just happy to be participating myself. It had been touch-and-go, my grades not the best for a college prep high school. I thought back to how I'd had to repeat a typing class. I thought to myself, "At least now I know how to type sixty words a minute."

I drove with a hint of nostalgia for the last four years. I'd had a great high school experience. I'd remained on friendly terms with everyone in my class. I wasn't a nomad. I enjoyed friendship, popularity, and acceptance. I thought that it was ironic that Cindy Lauper's song, "Girls Just Want To Have Fun" was playing on my car radio. The song was perfect to describe my life in high school.

When the photographer asked, "Are all the students here?" I replied, "My friends aren't here yet. They're fashionably late."

A couple of minutes later, when the photographer was given the green light to take the photo, he said, "Say cheese!"

One of the students yelled, "Class of '82 rules!" The crowd laughed loudly. It was the last laugh that we would share together.

I walked proudly down the church aisle. I glanced over at my mother, who appeared to have taken my advice to arrive early. She had a great seat for taking pictures of me when I received my diploma. I glanced at Cindy. She had a pillow in her hands. I thought to myself, "Why is Cynthia carrying a pillow to a graduation ceremony?"

The pillow had words on it that I could barely decipher. I read the word, "Europe" and thought that my mother was going to take another trip abroad with Maurice. I didn't want to think about my mother disappearing again for a month. I took my diploma and went back to my seat. Cynthia turned around, and I tried to mouth the words, "Is my mom going to Europe?"

Cynthia looked at me and pointed. I thought I saw her say, "You are."

The ceremony was impressive, and because we were in God's house, I felt religious emotions. I sat through many masses trying to instigate laughter from my friends, but I felt like I'd received redemption that day. I felt that even though I sinned my way through high school, God was showing me that he was divine. When I walked out of the large, wooden door of the Church, my mother greeted me with "I'm proud of you. I love you. I want you to have this pillow."

I looked at the beautiful white eyelet pillow, knowing that it was handmade by my mother. I read the blue velvet wording that said, "Pam '82, Europe for You!" I started to cry. I knew at that moment that there was a God. He had a plan for me. God amazed me. My mother and I looked at each other. I whispered, "Thank-you" as I gave her a big hug. I knew that I no longer had any resentment toward my mother. The experience of the divorce, my mother's penny-pinching ways, even the lack of parental guidance, was a turning point that could possibly have a good ending. I knew that my mother loved me. This trip to Europe had been carefully planned and paid for, even when I didn't deserve such an extravagant gift. She never stopped thinking about her shy daughter who wanted the moon. My life's events had seemed misguided, but I would now experience something that my mother had only dreamed about at my age. She was determined to create a path that would take me miles from the road she herself had traveled, helping me become mature through seeing the world.

CHAPTER SIXTEEN
SCRUPULOUS

The day after my birthday, I picked up the phone groggily. On the other end I heard a familiar voice saying, "Bill's dead. He died early this morning. I'll call you later with more details."

I was screaming and in tears by the time I got to my mother's room, yelling, "Bill's dead. Bill's dead."

My mother sat upright in bed, and all she could say was, "What! How'd he die? Was he at work? Who told you this? Oh my God—if you wouldn't have been with us in Santa Barbara for your birthday you would've possibly been with him! Thank God!"

I looked at my mother and said, "Mother, how can you say such a thing?"

Bill had come home late from a party. I heard through the grapevine that his girlfriend had called home and asked her parents if she could stay the night at Bill's because they had come from a party where alcohol was served. It was two in the morning and her mother wanted Bill to drive her home. The last decision Bill made that night was to take his girlfriend's VW bug. He left his Jeep Renegade, equipped with its protective roll bar, in his familiar parking space. That impulsive decision, like the decision to eat the strawberry pie, had a phenomenal impact on those who knew him.

If time could "rewrite every line" what would those words say? I learned from the experience of losing a loved one that every decision we make has an effect on someone else's life. We may not know this when we're making decisions, but in one way or the other, we are affecting others. When Bill decided to eat the strawberry pie, he suffered the consequence of losing his job. That decision affected those around him. When Bill lost his job, he was unable to contribute money to help pay the rent. Not only was he affected, but his mother was affected in some way, too. Bill was lucky in that he was able to find a better-paying job. In finding another job, a better-paying job, Bill was able to buy a nice car. He met the girl who was with him when he died through a co-worker. She was the co-worker's sister.

Bill made a decision that night that would affect everyone he knew. He had only lived in Ventura for a short time. In that time, he made many friends. He was gregarious and charming with everyone he came into contact with. I loved Bill. One thing that I hadn't fully realized was that a lot of other people loved him, too. He touched people in a way that I have never been able to understand. Bill's legacy has remained forever in my heart, even though in the end he hurt me deeply.

One thing that I have had a difficult time understanding when I reflect is that I never got to officially say good-bye to Bill. He left a deep imprint on my heart: after more than twenty years, I still think about Bill from time to time. Not only was he my first love, we never formally broke up. It seemed to me that he was able to overcome the hurt of his own parents' divorce and his mother's addiction.

Bill fell asleep at the wheel 175 feet south of Woodland Avenue, a street located adjacent to Highway 33. Bill was another victim of a traffic accident—he was DOA on the way to Ojai Valley Hospital. He died on June 24, 1982, the day after my eighteenth birthday. Bill's funeral was standing room only.

If I didn't have the trip to Europe to distract me, the shock from that phone call would have had a profound impact on my life. Perhaps I would not have been as scrupulous as Bill had been by obeying his girlfriend's parents' wish to have her home that night. I knew that God was with me every moment of my senior year in high school. It was by God's grace that I was able to graduate from high school and survive the emotional impact of my parent's divorce as well as Bill's death. My mother told me that morning, when I went crying and screaming into her bedroom after the phone call, "God has plans for you, Pamela, even though you don't know it yet. God took Bill away from you long before he died, so that your pain and suffering would be less. One thing I know, no matter how many others I've been wrong about, is that—all of the days of my life—I'll thank God you weren't in the car with Bill that night. God has given you a different path, one that includes getting away from here for a while. You'll grow mentally, spiritually, and emotionally."

On the way to Europe, I tried to relax on the plane, leaning back in my window seat. I looked down at the beautiful sea, Bill's new resting place. Rudy had assisted Margaret in throwing his ashes off of the Ventura pier into the beautiful Pacific Ocean, the scene of so many precious experiences and memories. I knew that my first love would live on—if not in the sea below, in my heart forever.

EPILOGUE

Twenty years after Bill's death, I was walking on Main Street in the old downtown area of Ventura. I stopped walking and explained to my daughters, Alice and Kaitlyn (my son, William John, was down in San Diego at Sea World Camp), "Let's go inside this old bookstore. I want to get a couple books."

I didn't know why I wanted to get a couple of books. I don't even know what type of book I was looking for. *Ghosts of the Ojai, California's most Haunted Valley,* a book by a man named Richard Senate, caught my eye and piqued my curiosity. I picked it and started reading. A chapter titled, "The Black Dog of the Ojai" was fascinating. One sentence took me by surprise. The sentence reads, "Those driving late at night in Ojai have seen a large dog running along the road." Apparently, "if you make the sign of the cross before the dog pounces, you have one chance to escape destruction." Needless to say, I also purchased the book titled, "Ventura: Mystic City by the Sea" by Maurine Moore. Both of the books explore the area's "haunted legacy."

I may never have my questions answered as to what happened to Bill. Did he die in a drunken driving accident, or did he simply fall asleep at the wheel? Was the Ventura area haunted? Did a large black dog cross in front of Bill when he was driving? One thing's for sure, I will be conscious of every decision that I make in life.

As I was writing this book, I made a conscious choice to look in an old wooden box where I stored my keepsakes. Like the books in the Ventura bookstore, I was drawn to the box after all of these years without knowing quite why. I opened it and found the golden promise ring that Bill had given me so long ago. I took my finding the ring as a reassuring reminder that the events had actually happened, and that I had had a first love experience. I still had the ring after all those years. The ring symbolizes a life of love, family, and prosperity ... a life that Bill had promised me I'd have, even though he wasn't part of the promise. I've made a conscious choice to keep the promise ring out in plain view so that I can reflect on the choices and decisions I make today and in my future. To me the promise ring symbolizes choices.

I have always had concerns about rejection and betrayal, especially after Bill deceived me. Because of my parents' divorce, I am at higher risk for conflicts in my interpersonal relationships. I hope that a conscious decision to divorce would include gathering statistics and information. I encourage parents to attend workshops and classes to help their children cope. The major factor in my life as a teen whose parents divorced was lack of parental involvement in my schoolwork and personal relationships. Statistics show that teenagers whose parents are divorced have a much higher incidence of sexual promiscuity. I encourage parents to put their children first when going through a divorce, because for kids, interpersonal relationships could end badly, having a life impact. Hopefully this book has given you some insight into how interpersonal relationships and everyday choices can affect your life.

I would like to thank my mother, whom I now consider my best friend. Her courage and love have guided me in life and in the writing of this story.

978-0-595-41842-8
0-595-41842-2

Printed in the United States
91328LV00005B/369/A